ROMEO,
JULIET &
HITLER

ROMEO, JULIET & HITLER

... can he put brakes on love

Rohan Gautam

Srishti
PUBLISHERS & DISTRIBUTORS

SRISHTI PUBLISHERS & DISTRIBUTORS
N-16, C. R. Park
New Delhi 110 019
editorial@srishtipublishers.com

First published by
Srishti Publishers & Distributors in 2014

Typeset by Eshu Graphic

Dedicated to my Mother
Who shelters in heaven

CONTENTS

ACKNOWLEDGEMENTS

When my Father heard that his son has written something which could get published, he was not ready to believe it. So, I acknowledge him first to make him a highly proud father. Papa, I hope now you are puffed up.

Efforts of my brother Rohit Gautam are not ordinary in getting this book written. His unabated interest for months played a winning role in my work. My sister Shweta will kill me if she doesn't get to see her name on this page. But seriously she was a huge help throughout.

Others equally important would be, Purnendu and Sudhanshu Chaubey, my uncles, for giving their gigantic support. I have equally big reason to thank the new person in my family, Sangeet Mani Shukla, my sister's husband, and more so for allowing me to use his laptop at times when mine ditched.

Friends – Satish Singh, Deepali Mooray and Amit Dagar. It was never possible to write this book without them being on my side, especially Saurabh, who is such a freak. I know he would not mind me calling him that.

Lastly, I am indebted to my publisher Srishti; they made the train reach the destination, and made me an author.

And lastly, again, YOU, the reader of this book.

PROLOGUE

My friend Saurabh drove me as fast as he could to Varanasi railway station. He had driven his Maruti 800 as if it were a Ferrari and I feared losing my life as a result of a spine-chilling display of his driving. My train for Delhi was at 6:30 in the evening; the square watch on my wrist suggested that I had precisely five minutes to make a successful boarding, though, there was no chance at all that I could even see the train anytime sooner than ten minutes, no matter how madly we rushed. When I began climbing the stairs of the station, it was clearly past 6:30. Saurabh remained in his car; he was injured in his leg due to which he could only crawl like a tortoise, and I needed to run like an athlete to catch my train.

Our chase proved to be unsuccessful; the train was gone. This was the first time I had missed a train. I put my bag back on my shoulder and walked back to the parking, like a loser. Saurabh was waiting; He had not left because even he knew it quite well that he would have to drop me home. I opened the door of the car in frustration, slammed it on getting in.

"You missed it?" He had never sounded so irritating to me. His sweetly-asked question only worked to aggravate my anger.

"No, actually a mad dog bit me and I came back dancing after reaching halfway," I said in exasperation.

"Freak! You just can't do that," he said with enough seriousness.

"Exactly can't as I am not bitten by a mad dog. The fact is you are an asshole and that's why I missed my train." I spoke in a style too theatrical.

"Hey look, I am sorry man!"

"Oh sorry... I see..." I continued my theatre performance.

"You go to your girlfriend's place, Pooja right?" He nodded. "Ok you go to her place just to impress her mother. There, her mother is taking the pet out for its routine pee, you force her into allowing you to take the pet out, ignoring the fact that it is a German Shepherd. Your own pet is not even an ordinary dog; you hide from the world that you have a cat as a pet!"

"Hey, don't you drag Sanjana into this." He protested. Sanjana is his cat of course and Sanjana is more like a female member of his family.

"Shut up! Then you do something weird, you try and check if it is a female dog or a male dog. The dog dislikes it, it runs after you. You reach the elevator which is actually of old style with channels. You clear the channels, without being sure of the lift on the floor. You take a step. There is a loud cry. You are down in to the lift base. You call me while I do my packing. I rush to you, take you to the hospital, you get 20 stitches. We get late and I miss my train."

"Man, not twenty, but eighteen," Saurabh corrected.

"Oh, whatever. I have a few questions... Why the hell were you trying to impress her mother? You tried that's ok! What made you feel you could find a way with a ferocious German Shepherd? You felt that's ok! What was the need of doing something so stupid? You stretched its back legs to check its gender? If you use your mind, it's visible from both sides. Let me not count it as a mistake. What was the point in taking the lift from the first floor, if a mad dog is behind your ass? In case you have a point how is this even possible that you simply jumped into the lift base?" I fumed like hell.

"Bro, I am sorry!"

"Oh, sorry again? Should I say all that again?"

"Man I was nearly dead!" he tried to tranquilize me using trickery, emotional trickery. My heart had to melt. He was as important to me as my family. I slowly took my eyes to his face, gave him a look that said "I will kill you asshole." He flashed his unbearably irritating smile. I patted his left thigh, mistakenly. He made a screech out of pain, and then ignited the car engine and now I did not feel bad, despite having missed the train. He accelerated and I was in a better mood.

"One thing is still not clear to me. Why were you trying to find out whether it was a male dog or a female dog?"

He gave me the look of an angry young man.

"Oh, I should know better. How lecherous you are!" I laughed noisily; he changed the gear and we reached home.

LOVE EXPRESS (VARANASI TO DELHI)

God does things in style and it is possible that he even cracks a laugh when he succeeds in his intentions of getting us perplexed. I really feel if God decides to build a career in film making, he will surely bag the prestigious Oscars at least for the best script category or best story. If no one else, then I would be the one to testify this farsightedness. In my case I am sure he was making a film in which I played the lead role. Because of a mentally sick friend I had failed to board my train and now I was going to catch a train to Delhi two days later.

Again I tugged the bag on my shoulders, touched my grandmother's feet and hugged her. I left; Saurabh had gone to the doctor for his injuries so this time he was not with me. My ticket wasn't confirmed but it was almost certain that it would fetch a seat for a comfortable journey. I reached the station, this time well before time. The whole platform was choked with passengers; I kind of struggled to move. There were all kinds of noises, of cooing babies, of aunties telling their husbands about their neighbor's new car, sofa, and other things, old people who mostly discussed their medical and of course kids who disturbed the elderly in everything. Among so many people I stood with my ears blocked in with earphones and I enjoyed Enrique Iglesias.

The train arrived at a low speed after someone made a lousy announcement. I have always wondered why Indian Railways can't have decent-speaking people to make the announcements in a proper way. Leave alone English, they even mess up with Hindi. I lifted my slightly heavy bag and when I thought about my coach, I realized my ticket had not been confirmed and I hadn't even bothered to check its confirmation status. For a couple of minutes I looked here and there, suddenly my eyes caught sight of a man with a black coat. I scurried towards him and tried to enquire about my coach and seat number. He gave me a dirty look. He was the wrong man, just a passenger like me. Not that the fault was mine, his attire made him fit to be a TC.

On asking a supposedly sane passenger who stood near me I came to know about a certain kind of board where tickets confirmation details were displayed. The next minute my eyes caught sight of a few people who alternated between looking at their tickets and a big wall-like board covered with thin sheets. I rushed towards them and tried to make my way to the board by pushing a few people.

I simply murmured my coach and seat number to make sure I remembered it at least till I reached my seat. I tugged my bag by my hand and turned back to finally head towards the train. As soon as I turned back, I found a moon-faced girl standing right in front of my eyes. She looked stunningly beautiful. She was a known face. She was Shreya. We were together in school for a few years. As far as I remembered, I had had just two short conversations with her during times of group activity or some such thing. She was the prettiest girl around in our school, sizzling and ravishing. And all the creatures in our school with testosterone had the hots for her. I liked her too. But I never felt any kind of urge to see her during lunch breaks while she talked to her friends in a group or during prayers when she solemnly prayed with folded hands. If love was some sort of electricity, my heart was very much a poor conductor in the language of science.

The guy who sat next to me in class was getting sleepless nights and I advised him to start using a mosquito net or an electronic mosquito killer as I was sure his problem was a room full of mosquitoes. He looked at me in anger and said "Dude, I am in love". Another friend of mine had gone completely insane because he had started wasting most of his pocket money on cards and chocolates. One day I tried to make him realize that he had already got himself ripped off badly and now was the time to stop.But the next day he spent on costlier cards and chocolates. I was surely not one of those who sat at the first bench and listened to every word that spilled out of the teacher's mouth. Even I had crushes and used to be a popular guy among girls. But love is an out of this world feeling; I had never felt it. I always thought it was something frivolous. Shahjahan must have liked Mumtaz, felt like going out on a date with her, planned marrying her and having babies. But hang on; he was a freak to get a wonder built for her. What would have been the condition of his heart when he decided to build the Taj Mahal for Mumtaz? Could his feelings be ever grasped? Let me answer, not until you fall in love.

Shreya was looking at me with her brown sparkling eyes. The last time I had seen her flawlessly beautiful face was a year ago. I was holidaying in Varanasi; a friend had organised a small get-together of old classmates at a ghatside garden restaurant. Shreya had made an appearance too. I still remember how serene her pretty face had appeared to me. She was dressed in black that complimented her spotless white complexion. I had found her amazingly gorgeous when we had sailed on a boat in the Ganges. She had sat right next to me in the wooden boat and I had fixed my gaze on her. And here she was, in front of my eyes, with the same divine beauty.

"Shreya!" I fumbled.

"Rohan? You were here in Varanasi?"

"Yeah I came here last week to enjoy my vacation and today I am going back. And you?" The last word came out of my mouth with much curiosity.

"My brother works in Delhi and I visit him every month." She articulated. I noticed her eyes blinked with the same pace as she spoke. Abruptly, she checked the silver watch on her hand and said, "Let's hurry, the train is about to depart."

What's your coach number?" She enquired.

"AS 1," I mumbled.

"Now that's the pinnacle of coincidence. You are going to share your coach with me."

"That's great!" I said.

"That means you will have to bear with some disturbance," she said with laughter while we boarded the train. We both laughed. My mind was full of thoughts. I thought about all my past journeys by train and concluded I barely had such an amazing fluke before. Rather all my past train experiences had been ordeals. As soon as we got inside the train, Shreya stopped near a lady who I thought was perfectly fit for a role in Ekta Kapoor's daily soap. Her face was composed and immobile.

I stood astounded for a few seconds when I found myself being introduced to her by Shreya, "Rohan, my school friend." She whispered and I scrambled out of my perplexed state as I realized the lady was Shreya's mother. I was taken by great surprise when she introduced me as her friend. It was a false introduction for sure; we had never been close enough to be called 'friends'.

Her mother kept a neutral expression while Shreya introduced me.

"Hello," I said followed by a shy smile. I headed towards my seat as I smiled half a smile looking at Shreya. I barely felt any comfort in front of her mother and soon I rushed towards my seat. It was the side window seat and as I sat I realized the seat right in front of me was empty.

I looked in the direction of their seats with curious eyes, hoping for Shreya to come and join me herself. The eagerness to know her, to talk to her, was soaring in me. But there was no sign of her approaching me. I switched my I-pod on, hummed the song that played and shut my eyes in order to rejuvenate myself. Every bit of my mind was still captured by the thoughts of Shreya. I had just lingered for a few minutes in that posture when I was hideously distracted by a pantry man whose extra loud voice that said "Nescafe" ruined my out of the ordinary nap. I opened my eyes in slow and steady motion along with impending lines on my forehead. Once my eyes were back to active I found someone on the seat right in front me. Who else could it be? She was the one for whom I had waited and eventually dozed off – Shreya.

Shreya adjusted her brownish hair at the back of her head. For a moment, I thought I was merely hallucinating before I realized it was indeed Shreya.

"I am sorry, these pantry people are so loud," she said.

"No, that's okay when did you come and why didn't you wake me up?" I sounded much faster than I had wanted.

"Just a few minutes back. I wanted to, but you seemed to enjoy your sweet nap so I refrained." She said nonchalantly. (I wondered if she knew she was the sole thought in my sweet nap as well.)

"It was certainly quite refreshing." I admitted with a shy smile as I thought over what I said.

"So I am sure you made the most of this trip?" She asked as she looked into my eyes with higher intensity.

"Not really, just dilly-dallied, didn't quite hang out with friends. Yeah I didn't miss to go to the Ghats," I answered as my gaze entered deeper into her eyes. She scrutinized my eyes as she broached the subject of my mother's demise; it had been six months since she had passed away. My eyes suddenly fell as my whole mood changed.

"It must have been so difficult, but what caused her death? she asked

I spent a few seconds looking here and there; I always needed strength to talk about that pain.

"That day she woke up with fever, we thought it was nothing but just some common fever. She had been on bed taking rest and then when she got up to go to the loo, she fainted. I ran and held her in my arms while my father phoned his doctor friend. Unfortunately, he was out of town so we rushed her to the hospital. She remained there for a few hours and she seemed to be getting better." After a pause I spoke again, "Doctors declared her fine; it was just a minor stomach infection. We brought her home; and while taking rest she called all of us. She looked at me with those eyes as if she was seeing me for the last time. Her breath became abnormal, and then there was no movement in her. We rushed back to hospital but…" Now I had no words to say, my voice choked. It was quite unusual on my part to talk about my anguish with someone I was barely close to. It was the kind of grief about which I had never spoken to anyone, not even to those who were always around me. Shreya remained silent for a few minutes; I needed those minutes of silence anyway. She observed I had escaped into a world where I was full of my miseries and despair. She leaned forward to look into my eyes.

She tried to meet my eyes as she said, "Rohan, not even in my imagination I can extinguish your pain. I know how unbearable it is. But one thing I would definitely say, who knows what lies after death? It is very much possible that the soul of our beloved continues to remain with us. I am sure you know that the soul never dies. The human body is mortal but the soul is immortal. So there is a good chance that she can see you at this moment. So will you make her feel terrible with your sad face?"

I shook my head. Her voice was so tranquil. I wondered whether the way I had seen a goddess talking in a devotional soap was any different. I was attuned to people's condolences and sympathies, but she said things that really eased out my pain. No one had ever said those things to me before. I felt like believing in her, in every word that she said, and I was clearly doing it as I scrambled out of my sorrowful world unbelievably.

"Thanks!" I mumbled. Her flawlessly drastic effort to turn things blissful was hard to believe.

"But still, there is no smile on your face," she complained.

"Sorry," I said. My throat was too full to speak. I had to clear it off well by controlling the tide of emotions in me. Taking myself out of such cheerless thoughts so quickly had never been an easy task. Once I got soaked in the pain of my past, everything around me appeared haggard and meaningless. Shreya made the job easier for me by taking the lead as she ignited the conversation between us; I had still been too solemn to be able to utter a single word.

"Do you miss our school days?" she questioned with much ardor as if she intended to fill me up with a bit of excitement. Her tone was quite chirpy.

"Of course, I miss those days. I miss every bit of school," I answered in a tone that suggested my mood was surely improving.

"And it was so terrible that despite being classmates we never happened to be friends." Her tone was remorseful. Her baby face was miraculously beautiful. My coherence was draining out so speedily that it took me a few seconds to restore it and respond to her.

"Hmmm... right. But I remember those few occasions when we did talk and I had no idea that you would be so good in talking." I spoke the words followed by a smile. My voice was getting louder without doubt. In spite of my efforts to sound normal, I continued losing my sanity at frequent intervals. I found her enthusiasm mounting as we got deeper into the conversation. My eyes repeatedly strayed onto her but I made sure she didn't have a clue of it.

The next few minutes passed in talking about our respective lives and how they were moving. I told her about my altered life in Delhi and how I had grown used to it steadily. She listened to me with enough interests and curiosity. The expression on her face varied with my words. The pressing of her lips, rolling of eyes, rising of eyebrows were the best among her expressions. It was causing a drug like effect on me. Once I finished speaking, inadvertently I turned nosy and started making efforts to know more about her life. Soon I gathered that there was something which hampered the light of her eyes. The sudden change in her eyes signaled that she was despairing; I could say she was fretting over something .

"I am repenting the fact that I was born in a doctor's family. Ever since I was born, my father started nourishing dreams of seeing me as a doctor. As I grew out of my adolescence, I was unsure about what I wanted from life. But now I know what fills my heart with excitement and ardor. I have a strong desire to be a fashion designer. I have assisted a boutique owner and even she strongly feels I have this talent. I dared and spoke about it to my father. He simply laughed at me." Her tone was full of sadness. She further informed me about her failure in cracking any MBBS entrance for two years. She hung her head in total sadness. I waited a few seconds until it dawned on me that I was required to make a move. It was my turn now to remove that covering of sorrow from her heart. I looked here and there but nothing came to my mind while Shreya's face still looked grumpy. I had never performed such a task before in life, the task of handling a beautiful girl when she was disconsolate. Time was running out and I wanted my timing to be as perfect as the timing of Bollywood heroes. The hero is always close to the heroine at the time of her need and only that makes the heroine fall for him. Imagine the case when the hero is late and the bad man has already left after playing with heroine's duppatta publicly, or the thief running away with the heroine's purse is far beyond the reach of the hero. Now here hero cannot dream of a happy married life with the heroine because he missed it.

After hearing a big 'come on' that came from inside me,. I asked her, "Do you think your father loves you?"

She looked into my eyes and said, "Yes".

"So it's highly unimaginable that such a father would ever steal the happiness of his daughter. You just got to attack his emotions and I am sure you will get him on your side. All I am asking is that you act like a daughter." I exerted faintheartedly. As soon as I finished saying this, I made an attempt to observe her face to see if I had made any difference. And as a matter of delight for me, the difference was clear; that glitter had returned to her eyes. Having managed to cheer up a beautiful girl, which was not an easy job for me, I felt like "the Badshah Sharukh Khan".

"Thanks! I think it has been my fault only as I never convinced him the way I should have." Now in my mind I was overjoyed; somehow I had managed to give her hope. The next few minutes passed in silence. We both realized the need of silence for a few moments. Shreya rested her head on the window pane. She appeared expressionless while she gazed out of the window, though hardly anything was clearly visible. The sun was still to set, and it glistened on Shreya's face through the black window pane, providing a golden glow to it. I rummaged into my bag and emerged with a short story book as I didn't want to sit clumsily and lost, facing a girl who caused tingling of my spine every time I looked at her face. I started flipping through the pages of the book, struggling to conceal my desire that demanded my eyes to be on the girl who sat in front of me. What in this world was going to hold my interest better than gazing at this beautiful creation of God? I decided to allow myself a look at Shreya again. I raised my head and now I found her working on her nails in an attempt to give them a better shape. I pondered if there was any room at all for improvement, they were already very beautiful. The moment I realized I was staring at her, I looked away, but by that time it was too late and our eyes met.

"It seems books are your best pals," she chortled. I was speechless for a few seconds with a shy smile showing up on my face. I opened my stuttering mouth without any word stored in it for a response.

"No, I was just..." I left the sentence hanging as I steadily kept the book beside me.

"You were just...?"

"I was just reading this short story... Ah...quite an interesting one!"

"So aren't you going to share your interesting story with me?" She demanded as her eyes narrowed and her upper and lower eye lashes kissed each other more frequently. I swallowed harder, struggling to come up with some story. I reached for my book quite discreetly as I couldn't think of any escape from those brown eyes.

"Hey hey... No classroom reading please. I want to hear your story in your own words," she said. Her eyes widened like an ocean this time.

"Of course... why not," I stammered.

"So let's get started," she said excitedly, elongating her dark pink glossy lips in a heart-stopping smile.

I summoned enough courage to open my mouth, but without any story with me. I was hardly reading any story.

"I don't think it will hold your interest," I said in a few broken sentences.

"Don't lie; you have already told me it's interesting. So there you go," she spoke with varying expressions.

Now I realized I had to think of something but it was as difficult as finding a bucket full of water in a desert at that precise moment. After taking a few seconds, I was struck by the idea of narrating her the story of some movie. Still there was risk in case she realized it was the story of a film and not an original one from the book. I chose to play safe: I picked an old movie and not a latest one.

After taking some five minutes to prepare myself, I opened my mouth.

"It's about two men – James and Victor, they are kind of thieves. Once they go to a village which is in fear of a man called Gabriel. James and Victor meet Taylor who is the village chief. Taylor persuades James and Victor to agree to fight Gabriel and free the whole village from his threat. And yeah, Taylor (the village chief) is a man with only one hand. Years ago his other hand was axed by Gabriel so it ends with James and Victor killing Gabriel. But sadly, James also gets killed fighting Gabriel." The story was over and now I breathed. Shreya was startled and I noticed she was controlling her laughter. The next moment she asked for my book and I gave it to her in diffidence. She gave a quick look to the page of contents and closed the book with a big smile.

"Rohan, there is no such story."

"There is… I am sure… I just read…" I fumbled. I said "shit" in my imagination.

"Dear, it just can't be because it was your own English remake of *Sholay* starring Amitabh Bachhan and Dharmendra," she articulated this time and laughed like mad.

"James for Jai, Victor for Viru, Gabriel for Gabbar Singh and Taylor for thakur? Very smart!" she said as she laughed hysterically. For me now was the time to surrender. I cursed myself for coming up with such a stupid story and preferred to join her in her laughter. We both laughed looking at each other, we laughed at regular intervals for an hour at my stupidity. I realized it was my most favuorite sound in the whole world, the sound of her laughter. She told me she had caught me flipping 3-4 pages together and then she had understood that I was not reading. I accepted it all in silence, though she did not pester me to know why I was pretending to read. Seldom had my flamboyance dumped me in that fashion. But had I realized it was the day when all peculiar things were occurring to me.

In the train, during those moments, I cursed myself for my moronic appearance. Why on earth did I have to pretend to be an earnest reader!

As I pondered over it, I risked another glance at her. Having stolen a few heart-stopping glimpses at her, I commanded my eyes to revert and not lose control, though in reluctance. Soon I regained some composure that made me realize, I definitely needed to get both my mind and heart under control. The track of time was lost, the clue whether it was day or night had been missing, and with that an unknown feeling was emerging and I was too lost to trace its source.

My breath soon got converted into hyperventilation. I felt something in my chest that made me gulp time and again. I was losing my mind, never had I felt so uneasy before. My blood had begun to run a lot faster than usual, my whole body vibrated. I slapped myself in my imagination, followed with an acrimonious speech. I will produce that drastic speech before you.

"Dude... what's wrong with you? What on earth makes you so damn nervous? Do you think this girl is going to eat you up? No, do you think this *very beautiful* girl is going to eat you up? I rectified my question. Oh! Hang on. Are you diffident because of her divine beauty?" I got no reply, no answer. There I was, with my reason behind behaving like a traditional Indian bride who hides her face behind a veil and weighs her words not less than a hundred times before speaking; who often dreads of a scolding also. During all my lecturing to myself, Shreya had talked to her brother over phone. I made myself understand that I lacked nothing, be it looks or style; I had it in me.

It seemed Shreya was about to finish her telecon. I needed to make an attempt to strike a conversation. As soon as she disconnected the call, she flashed a smile in my direction and I responded with a smile that looked like a smile this time. The glass of silence was broken as I asked her, "So, where are you going to put up in Delhi?"

My tone was not the way I had wanted it to be, I rued it as I had not wanted to emerge with a macho swagger, I simply wanted to scramble over my much pathetic condition.

"I think I have told you my brother lives in Delhi and I visit him every month," she replied in her soothing voice.

"That I know, but where in Delhi? I mean the location…" I said.

"Oh, I am sorry. Defence Colony." I tried to figure out if I had ever heard of this place before; the answer was a no. I was still very much an alien in the city. I barely knew it well.

"Helowww." She shook me out of my gloom. "Rohan, is your world more beautiful than this?" I was confused at what she had asked me.

"What?" I said quite baffled.

"Why? Don't you have a world of your own?" she asked.

"What world?" I stuttered.

"Do you remember our English teacher Mrs. Hussain who had once remarked that you have a world of your own and you remain in that world quite a lot?" she said with a smile.

"Yes," I replied in shock. I remembered quite well and so did she. But was it such a common possibility that she remembered it? And did she remember more of such remarks about me? Why did she hear all those remarks about me so attentively that she remembered it even after years?

"I know I am boring you." I admitted shyly.

"Till now, definitely yes," she said and laughed. But now I felt a sudden impulse, a strong desire to overcome my uncommunicativeness and talk to her the way I had wanted to. I glanced at my watch and it was already eight. Time was passing faster than ever and I badly wanted to live in the eccentricity of that moment.

Everything was just so perfect, beyond words, beyond any description. Generally, these trains are buzzing with people but miraculously not many eyes disturbed us; there were very few passengers around, our privacy was undisturbed. I had had no idea of a perfect date. If I envisaged one, a date in a train was the most unique. Dates in restaurants and parks were all very common. But who would call it a date; I was barely speaking. Anyone else in my shoes could have done better.

The train shoved as my heart functioned faster; we had come to a halt at Kanpur station .The platform looked appallingly squalid with passengers lying like corpses on the floor.

"Hey, I am bored of sitting for hours. Let's just straighten our legs by taking a quick walk. How does it sound?" She asked but too keen on hearing a yes. I blinked at my watch, five minutes had elapsed and I still had five minutes to go for a memorable walk with Shreya. We jumped down, walked the length of the train as we caught the attention of almost everyone on the platform. I was sure they were trying to figure out if we were love birds and honestly I had not felt bad guessing what they felt. I walked with gallons of pride, feeling she was all mine. I looked at her face over and over. I wished that our walk would never end. But it's a basic truth that every good thing comes to an end. While we rushed back to the train, her cell phone rang. She picked and I could not hear a word despite my best efforts, as she spoke too softly. My heartbeats fastened.

Was that supposed to be her boyfriend's call? Was she already engaged? I examined her face meticulously and attempted to figure out if she was really talking to her boyfriend. I could not succeed in my endeavor as she spoke in a very low voice. It created fear in me that I was falling for a girl who already had a boyfriend and I would end up getting beaten by him. Her phone buzzed again, she said it was her mom again and she needed to go. She said she would come back. One thing was clear, the previous call was from her mother; I felt relieved.

I realized I needed to pee only after she was gone. Beautiful girls have this unique prowess, I tell you; with them you barely pay attention to any other thing in this world, not even to the need of going to the washroom. In a flash, I was back on my seat. I looked at the vacant seat in front of me and imagined her to be still there. Some of the passengers had started having their dinner. It's always an early dinner on a train. Although there was nothing visible through the dark window glass, I still tried to look out. In my mind I had just thought about Shreya, the time that I had spent with her in the train and the time that I was going to get with her. I did not have to wait long as she got back shortly. As soon as she sat down, she offered me some chocolates. Her father had brought them from Chicago, she told me. I thought it was quite ironical, usually a boy gives chocolates to a girl and here I was taking them, so I was the girl. I had to accept this and I did with slight reluctance.

"What...you don't like chocolates?" she asked surprised.

"I do like, but it's quite unusual … a guy taking chocolates from a girl. Usually, it's the other way round." I didn't know how I managed to speak up what I felt inside. This time she smiled pressing her lips harder. She looked at me with a lot of intensity and made me think about what I had said.

"Rohan, that's a girlfriend boyfriend thing...," she said and smiled.

"But anyway, do you have a girlfriend?" she asked. I was baffled by her question. I couldn't believe my ears at what she had asked me. I was going to have to take it as one level passed. Anyway, I did not want to make an eager announcement to her, nor did I have the intention to tell her my status. But somewhere in my heart there was a strong desire to convey that I was very much single. I never bought chocolates for anyone, never felt the need of buying something like a rose or a greeting card. Instead of giving her the answer right away, I preferred to talk more as I was trying to work on my communication skills.

"What do you think?" I questioned to know what was on her mind.

"Well, you live in a city full of hustle and bustle... You have spent two years in college already. Moreover these days girls are so crazy, I feel yes," she replied with a twisted expression.

"Oh, crazy," I said and laughed, she waited for the answer. "Sorry, no crazy girl has met me till date," I said as I laughed more.

"Why?" she asked in a soft voice and with a beautiful expression. She looked highly interested. I thought for a minute, looked at the floor of the train and then answered. "Perhaps because I have a world of my own and I mostly remain in it." I said and our eyes remained fixed at each other. I felt happier after I told her that I was very much single and available. Now was the chance to ask about her. She had already asked me so I could easily ask her, but I chickened out again. My heart was ready but my mouth was not ready to utter the words asking her if she was single. I looked around and most of the people slid down to lie on their seats for the night. Night was falling but I had just wanted to sit like that, facing her. The eccentricity of the night was easily felt by my heart and soul. All corners of my heart were occupied by thoughts about Shreya. I looked at her and could not stop myself from thinking if this serendipitous journey, by any chance, could be meaningful. Shreya realized it was time for dinner and she forced me to join them. I refused, though it was a good offer as I wasn't even carrying my dinner. But her mom, when I would be with her I would get conscious of the fact that I liked her daughter and that would make me nervous. She asked me if I would sleep late. I told her I wasn't at all sleepy, not even a bit sleepy. Though I wanted to say I would not sleep for the whole night, rather see you, hear you and be with you. Now she would come after dinner. I realized I was starving when she was not around. I caught hold of a pantry guy and asked him like a hero to bring a plate of food for me. He snapped me saying it was pretty late for placing an order. Suddenly that hero felt like a beggar, as it was the time to beg. I told him I was going to die in case I didn't get anything to eat; I made my face like a roasted brinjal. Thankfully he was convinced and I had my food for the night. I even ate like a beggar in the end. After dinner I waited for Shreya, with mixed feelings of desperation and curiosity. An hour passed and then the second, I sat in darkness, almost all the lights were off by now.

I couldn't control myself from going to see her at her seat. As soon as I reached there, I became a little nervous and then my eyes fell on her mother who slept on the lower berth. I had looked out for the daughter and the sight of the mother was fearful. She was asleep but the fear in me made her face appear quite sinister. I took my eyes off her, raised my head and now that sight was beautiful. Shreya had been sleeping on the top berth, thankfully in a position that allowed me to see her face quite easily. In all darkness, a beam of light reached her face and made it look like an angel's. Her hair was scattered all over her fair face, even her lips were not free room. I wanted to clear her face off with my fingers. I could have happily accepted any punishment by any court of India if it was a crime. My eyes went back to her mother on noticing her move slightly, and when her movement stopped I concentrated on Shreya again. What happened next was horrifying. Her mother was slowly getting herself into a sitting position, and I noticed that quite late too. For a second I thought I had landed myself into a big trouble. But I sighed when I learnt that she had still not seen me which was surely a matter of luck. Her eyes were on the brink of opening and I vanished like a fart in the wind. I walked hastily and stopped near the toilet area near two policemen who were on their routine checks. They looked at me with sharp eyes, suspecting me of being a thief, and using my eyes I made a desperate attempt to convince them that I wasn't. Shockingly, their eyes hardened on me and now my heart became a warehouse of fear. I would not hide my feeling,

I find policemen quite scary. Thanks to our Indian cinema that projects policemen as monsters. While they continued to look at me, I entered the toilet and breathed as if I had just saved my life. After spending five minutes inside I finally came out and the policemen were not there. I felt like taking some fresh air so I landed on the coach entrance. Now, I could see the sky and it was amazingly decorated with stars, the air smelled fresh and its force was highly enjoyable. I closed my eyes while the strong wind embraced me. That white face partly covered with a few long strands of hair still shone beautifully in my closed eyes. I was losing my inner peace; Shreya had ruined it all in a few hours. The night got lovelier every time my eyes imagined her face. My mind was soaked in thoughts of Shreya, thinking of the time that I had spent with her, thinking what life could be like with a girl like her. Shreya had been asleep which meant I was not going to get any more time with her. Minutes passed in a unique feeling, and I felt like seeing her face again. But I knew the risk involved. I reached my seat and with the feeling of a little cold, I lay down with a blanket covering me. It was so late in the night; still, I was far from being knocked out by sleep. The thought of Shreya was disturbing me. I was getting deeper into her thoughts. An hour passed, unconsciousness caused by a little sleep could not keep Shreya away from my heart and head. It was like I had been on a ride of love which was flipping me out badly. It continued for another one hour and slowly I dozed off to sleep. Suddenly there was a whispering sound which I heard only when it got a little louder. My unconscious brain turned active, the first thought it produced was about those two policemen who had threatened me with their hostile eyes. In reflex I lifted my upper body on my hands and the words that came out of my mouth were, "Look, I have done nothing." My eyes still got no clear picture and I repeated my words.

"Hey it's me… Are you ok? What happened?" Now that was a pure female voice. It had to be Shreya. I was stunned; Shreya looked frightened.

"I am ok… but what are you doing here?" I said, pleasantly surprised, though still in mild shock.

"I woke up for a few gulps of water and I thought of checking if you were asleep. I am sorry to have disturbed you."

"No, you did not," I said quickly, lest she decided to turn around and walk away.

"You scared the hell out of me. What was that? Nightmares?" she questioned. After spending a few seconds in silence, I accepted it was a nightmare. The same minute it struck me, the whole world would call me a fool if I wasted all my time. She sat with her legs on the floor and I remained fully on my seat. But Before I could say anything, she told me she needed to go. She was right. In case her mother woke up and found her daughter missing, it could get both of us killed. She stood up to go.

"See you in the morning," she said and I repeated the same. There was nothing I could do; she began to walk away. I was moaning from inside, it was painful. Now I just wanted a couple of hours to pass and the sun to show up again, for I would meet her in the morning. I tossed on my seat for the next few minutes before I drifted into sleep. Shreya was no doubt awake in me.

Chai, chai, chai, chai. Chaiwalas woke me up this time. I checked my watch; it was already 7:30. Most of the passengers around me were sipping their tea and eating sandwiches. When travelling by train, 7.30 am seems like too late. Delhi was just a few stations away but, there was hardly any sign of Shreya. Maybe she was still sleeping. I left my seat in a hurry to go to the wash basin to splash water on my face and a quick hair styling with my hands. Within no time I was back on my seat. Time was running out, needless to say I had been feeling something for her since the moment we began talking in the train. I was craving to talk to her. My desperation had started to freak me out again. Sitting and waiting for Shreya was becoming an impossible task. Had I shown some courage, I would have reached her seat; but call it shyness or cowardice, I was frozen on my seat. But if one avoids doing exercise or labor, one can't achieve success in love in the modern day world. An idea just popped up in my mind. It was a freaky idea but when you are in love, you become a freak. A chai wala just passed by, I bent right and the moment he reached closer to Shreya's seat, I screamed *chaii*. My voice echoed. Everyone around me, even those seated quite far, stared at my angrily. I had just banged on their eardrums terribly. I had to apologize softly saying "morning tea is so important," followed by sorry and then looking up and down, left and right and then up and down. Now I prayed I was loud enough to be heard by Shreya; my seeing her depended on that. The suspense of the moment could easily be related to an India-Pakistan cricket match, particularly the last over situation when the game is so well-balanced that any team can win. Of course, India winning the match would tantamount to Shreya coming to me. A few minutes passed and now I was full of cynicism. I told myself, "In the worst case, I would go to her". The case was indeed worst, I concluded that the effort went down the pan and I got up. The distance between us was as short as a ten-second long walk. After taking a few nervous steps towards her seat, I suddenly stopped as I saw Shreya. She had walked with her head down so I took an about turn and raced back to my seat. Now was the time my happiness returned to me, I clenched my fist and punched the air for my victory. A fat woman, who had earlier thrown an angry look at me for my mad act, saw my doing that and her expression suggested she was sure that I suffered from some mental disorder. I was a psychopath for her.

"So you got your cup of tea?" The moment she stopped at my seat, she asked this question. She looked really fresh like a flower with her open hair which fell beautifully on her shoulder. I was so mesmerized that I even forgot the trick which I had used a short while ago to bring her to me.

"What tea? I don't have a taste for tea," I said mindlessly.

"But I guess it was your voice calling that pantry guy for tea," I heard a loud ring and regained my mind.

"Oh ya ya, that was me. Actually my throat is terribly ruled by cough at the moment, so I thought tea would help," I fabricated.

"Oh, I have got cough tablets in my purse, I will just get it," she offered. I waved my hand to stop her but she was gone. Of course, I needed no cough tablets, I was fit and fine physically. I regretted and hit my fist on my forehead. Then I thought what a caring girlfriend she would make, actually a caring life partner. Thankfully she was back with me in a snap with some cough tablets.

"So you had a good sleep?" she asked.

"Oh yes, quite good," I said, but this was not an honest answer.

"Hope there were no nightmares later," she laughed and I smiled for the incident last night. Soon we realized Delhi was just minutes away. This beautiful journey had come to its end. She would be gone soon, when would I see her beautiful face again, or if there was actually no chance of seeing her ever again, would it again happen that we would share a laugh together? I had no answers for any of these questions. I had grown sentimental. While I contemplated I noticed she was looking at me. And now we both looked at each other in silence. That silence was quite meaningful; something was happening in that silence but it was beyond words.

"I will always remember this journey," I spoke in a low voice. She just half-smiled at that and said nothing. So far she had been talkative and all of a sudden she was silent. We spent some time gazing at each other.

"You don't wish to take my number?" she asked. My reaction on this was a mixture of embarrassment and anger at myself.

Without wasting a second, I gave her my number. It was a great devastation to see my own phone dead with empty battery. Quite hastily I reached for my bag to find a charger. I searched for it madly but failed. I had forgotten to keep it in my bag. When I raised my head after giving up, I was taken by enormous surprise. Shreya held a tissue and a pencil which was actually the kajal that she had used. She wrote down her number using that kajal on the tissue and gave it to me. I took it, too numb to say anything. We heard some passenger's voice announcing that Delhi was the next station. People around us had begun arranging their luggage. We both got up; I felt the pain of the moment, the pain of parting. I tried hard to make sure that my face remained without a sign of pain. Her face was totally unfathomable. I offered my right hand and she hers, we shook hands.

"Ok, see you," I said, my eyes turning serious.

"See you soon," she replied as she began to step back. That was the bye-bye moment, we both waved at each other. She was walking away from me and I was not ready to take my eyes off her. Before getting out of my sight, she looked back at me. I had already fixed my gaze on her, our eyes met and that happened without any expectation from my side. In that moment I felt like Shahrukh khan of DDLJ; surely that was a positive indication. If you have seen DDLJ even a single time then you are made to believe that if a girl turns back to look at you, that's an indication that she feels for you. Thanks to the makers of DDLJ, I felt jubilant now.

The train arrived at the New Delhi railway station. On the platform we both waved at each other, ignoring her mother. She was going away and I badly wanted to stop her from going. In complete pain I looked at her till she was finally out of my sight. The time spent in the auto rickshaw was not easy; I was sort of unconscious in her thoughts.

I had been in a different world altogether, just needed a friend's reassurance that would tell me, *tujhe pyar hogya hai saaley*. Behavioral changes in me were very much clear; hours passed thinking about her in silence, and enough of silence would further result in willingness to talk about her. Love is a strange phenomenon; it makes you both silent and talkative. One feels like getting the attention of the whole world, giving hundreds of interviews the way celebrities do, and hitting the headlines. And then one does not feel like being disturbed by anyone. I phoned Saurabh and told him what had happened; it took me nearly an hour to do that. He got delirious when I told him the girl was Shreya.

"Dude, Shreya? That glam girl from our class! You got to be kidding me brother? You are so lucky, dude. Anyway... did you guys kiss each other? Of course, you had so much time, kissing is obvious. Did you...?"

"Shut up." I prevented him from saying a word more. "I love her...," I said quite seriously.

BACHCHAN, TENDULKAR, BUT NO ACCOUNTANT

At dinner table that night, my father asked me about my future plans as it was my final year of college. It was not actually a nagging question but a discussion about my career. Chartered accountancy is what he wanted his son to pursue and for the last two years he was hell bent on this. Despite this, I developed no interest in it; rather, I began to feel a taste for marketing which happened mainly because my uncle was doing pretty well by travelling around the globe to sell Indian cheese. Selling cheese or butter was not a challenging job at all, plus I always wanted a job that had the travelling aspect, so now I only hoped of being within the boundaries of a renowned college offering an MBA degree. Besides like everyone else, I had a dream of doing something really big in life, something that Tendulkar did, something that Amitabh Bachhan did. Unfortunately, after having spent more than twenty years on the planet I had still not discovered that one thing that riddled my heart with great amount of passion. Actually there was one thing I admit: I wanted to become a singer, a star. However, I could not sing at a place better than my bathroom. But hopes were still looming that one day I would find something interesting to do which would actually be something other than maintaining balance sheets and profit and loss account that I was doing in college. So doing CA was like putting kerosene on your dreams and burning it with a matchstick. That night when he tried to convince me saying his practicing Chartered Accountant friend was dealing with clients as big as Radisson and Hyatt, I told him my dreams were limited to enjoying their table dinner once a week.

"There is no accountant inside me. Sorry," I said with an apology that contained two things – arrogance and attitude. I went to my room after dinner. For a second I thought of calling Shreya but then I realized it was better to go with a text message. I typed "hey" and sent it to her. I waited for her reply quite frantically, but for hours when I received no reply, I dozed off.

BEGGED TO AFFORD BURGERS
AND FRIES

Next day I woke up a few hours late, the first word that came to my mouth was 'shit' after my eyes caught my cell phone that waited for me with an unread message for last two hours. I picked it hastily and checked, it was the message for which I had waited for so long, my heart beats went sprinting. The next moment, I was torn between two things, whether to call her or just reply through a message. I could not lie to myself; I yearned to hear her captivating voice. I took a few seconds to decide, and called her up. Trrrr, trrrr…, my heart was ringing along with the phone on the other side of the line.

"Sir you finally woke up?" She said in a happy tone. She had never called me sir before. I took a second and thought over it. When a guy calls a girl ma'am, surely there is something in his heart for the girl. More so, most of the boyfriends call their girlfriends ma'am to pamper them. So if a girl uses the word 'sir' for a guy then there has to be something in her heart too. Unfortunately, I was not her boyfriend yet. The outcome of my analysis had increased my heartbeat manifold; I smiled in silence without saying a word, so Shreya continued.

"Oh, my fault maybe I texted too early," she said. I wanted to say 'no' a thousand times, but she carried on.

"Hey today we gang up, I mean I, Shruti and Ananya. I hope you still remember them, Fatty and Chatty. Tag along if you have a few hours." Fatty as in Shruti, I had remembered her well because of her boldness and her weight in tons; I knew that she lived in Noida now. Chatty was Ananya, quite popular for her ability to make people cry with her senseless chattering. As soon as she told me this, I felt a sudden wave of happiness. Shruti and Ananya were of course like weeds, but I was overjoyed to know that I would get to see Shreya. My excitement provoked me to say I was very much in. Unquestionably, it's hard to manage excitement once you are in love. I had discovered that lately.

"Cool! Thn we'll meet at 2 in McDonald's at CP, and be on time. Don't repeat your school time habit today."

"No, no. I will be on time," I said. When the call got over I smiled a truck full of smiles. I tell you such smiles are indicators that you have fallen head on heels for someone: smile while lying on the bed, smile while sitting on a toilet seat, smile while you talk to your father (the worst of all), smile while your friends tell you that you behave in a strange way these days, etc. Love makes you a complete freak. In the middle of all amazing feelings, it struck me that I had no money and I could not even have asked my father as I had already drawn a lot extra from him for my Varanasi trip. I cursed Saurabh unstoppably in my imagination for making me spend on unnecessary things during my vacation. My mind had stopped working; I was meeting her in a few hours. All you guys with girlfriends would identify with the situation I faced. That day I realized the importance of money; without money one should never fall in love, but one has no control over love. I checked every part of my wallet; I found only a few hundred rupee notes, without any sign of a thousand or even a five hundred note. It was just sufficient to buy burgers and soft drinks for four people in McDonald's. Besides, there would always be some more expenditure. It was time to spread my hands before friends. I phoned Satish and Nitish (my college buddies) and they reluctantly made a petty donation in my favor after minutes of crying over their own beggarly condition. But now I believed I could easily save my face in front of those three girls. I tried every shirt of my wardrobe in front of the mirror and picked the one I thought looked the best on me. I was a good half hour before time at the decided place. My phone rang, the screen read "Shreya calling".

"Don't tell me you got late because you could not find your shoes on time," she said in her mellifluous tone. To hear her say that I got embarrassed and speechless; she had not forgotten that highly flimsy excuse that I would use every time I was late for morning school prayer.

"No no. Shoes were in place. I am quite on time," I kind of blabbered and controlled the embarrassment which was now touching the sky. My heart produced a few stormy beats in a row when she informed me that Shruti and Ananya were not going to join in as they woke up on a college assignment deadline in the hindsight. She sounded disheartened; I was elated. Not because she was disheartened of course, but for the fact that now I would have to pay only for two burgers and coke, with or without French fries. It didn't bother me at all after the much needed no show of fatty and chatty; clearly the cherry on the cake was going to be those few hours with her in person. She reached; she had put on a red top along with blue jeans, her hair tied up, ever so beautiful. She walked up to me with a broad smile on her face; I almost fainted at that sight. It seemed she would just pass me by with her indescribable beauty, but she was there to meet me and so she stopped to show me her irresistibly bubbly expression. We nodded together to enter the restaurant and inside we ran our eyes all over the sitting area, (actually she did, and I ran my gaze on her face). She pointed towards two vacant chairs that waited for us; we sat down and smiled at each other. She refused to eat anything when I first asked her. Then I made a lame attempt at humor by saying we needed something on our table to occupy it else we were going to lose it to those with trays full of food. She laughed and agreed so I brought burgers, coke and some fries. We talked for the next half an hour, I was surely doing better. I casually asked if she tried again to convince her father for allowing her to do fashion designing. She played with the straw in her glass of coke and said it was a very difficult job. She still lacked courage to really do that. For a second I contemplated if I was supposed to repeat all that I had said in the train to make her understand it was not really a rocky road but something very much possible.

It was my responsibility to handle the situation so I did. I told her what exactly she needed to do; in stronger words this time and then we shunned discussing it any further. For something disastrous she could have taken offence, had I spoken a word against her father by mistake. Saurabh, who regularly tried to analyze the behavior of girls to be able to impress them, had once shared his findings that girls are subject to quick mood swings. One can't understand how quickly they get worked up from complete calmness. So it would be like the end of all my dreams; she would slap me and walk away. I would finish the remaining coke and french-fries and leave after her, hiding my face from so many eyes that saw me getting beaten up by a girl in public. When I realized this, I preferred talking about other unimportant things like her favorite cartoon character as a kid, her favorite chocolate, if she believed in ghosts, etc. She answered all my questions laughingly.

"Hey, Bangla Sahib Gurudwara is at a small distance. I have an urge to go there," she said and waited for a yes in excitement.

"Bangla Sahib…?" I asked as I discovered some truth in my friend's findings, she was all excited at once from a complete peaceful state.

"Yes, we have pretty good time to make it. Hitler is picking me at six. I mean, my brother. So what say?" My visit to religious places had been confined to Hanuman temples so she was taking me to a new place.

"Let's not waste time then," I smiled and said. She stood up to leave with abruptness and I still remained on my seat.

She had half-eaten her burger and the fries were almost untouched. I had borrowed to afford all that and the fact was quite painful that it would all go into a bin.

"Come on, get up!" she commanded. I stood up thinking about fries and half the burger that she had wasted. While we moved out of McDonald's, she shocked me with this news that she was going back to Varanasi the next day. It was because of her father who had made a sudden plan to take her to Dehradun for reasons regarding her admission into a medical college; he had been trying for months. I really hated her father in that moment. He had been torturing my love so heartlessly.

"Rickshaw?" She screamed and found an auto rickshaw for us. I questioned my manliness; she had done my job here. The next moment I got infuriated after hearing what auto rickshaw guy demanded for that short distance. It was nearly double of my calculation. Any guy with less understanding of the situation would have consumed more time to figure out that he took advantage of the situation. A girl stood next to me, and he knew I wasn't going to haggle. I wished I could give him a whiff of my condition, he would have charged me nothing out of humanity. I simply cursed him in my mind, all the bad ones to be precise, he deserved. We got into the rickshaw; the weather was beautiful, ideal for a day like this.

"Hey, don't you think we have been travelling together for so long?" she said.

"O yes, train and then this auto rickshaw," I replied as I breathed heavily. On consuming a few seconds I realized she had said something deeper than what I had understood. I felt those words were said by her out of certain kind of feeling but it could also be something said casually. We reached. It was my first visit to a Gurudwara and we went inside matching our footsteps. It was surely a different world with her, so unique and different. I was lost to see how deeply she believed in God, it made me feel that God existed. That moment, my emotions had troubled me and my love for her multiplied manifold. As she prayed, I simply looked at her. In my prayer, I just conveyed my feelings to God that I needed the girl who stood next to me for all my life. We reached the *sarovar* inside and I was amazed to see it full of fishes that were visible on the surface. I splashed water on my face while she ran her fingers in the water. We looked at each other over and over. Then we silently sat on the stairs to rest our legs.

"Do you have anyone in your life?" I asked finally. She glanced up at me, then her eyes retreated.

"No and I never had anyone," she replied after getting my question right. Her 'anyone' obviously didn't mean people like her mom-dad, uncle-aunty, both maternal and paternal, grandparents, friends, pet, dog, or cat etc. So the girl had been single all the while. I let her use more words by being tightlipped.

"It's not easy to find someone truthful," she said. The word truthful buzzed into my ears like an alarm. I tried to figure out if I was truthful and the conclusion was upsetting. I always relied on lies in my daily life. I controlled my thoughts. If you find someone truthful then will you … I kind of half asked.

"I can't fall like a toy in someone's hand either," she answered candidly. I understood I had to cover a long distance in the pursuit of getting her and I was totally ready for it. We strolled together for a long distance before hiring an auto rickshaw to take us back to Connaught Place. This time I did not allow the auto rickshaw driver to open a big mouth for nearly double fare. She waited and I walked, only to plead with the driver to charge within limits. I could not have taken the pain of any more extravagance. She told me how wonderful she felt every time she visited the place. I heard every word said by her scrupulously and thanked her for making me experience something esoteric. With merely half an hour left with us, we reached Connaught Place.

"Hey, help me in choosing a book for tomorrow's journey. You see, I will have no one so talented around me to make stories and remakes," she said and met my eyes in a mysterious style. We laughed and stopped at a bookstall.

"So, there you go. Choose one for me!" She ordered with a smile. Now that was an opportunity, an opportunity to give her a vague hint of my turbulent heart. From piles of books on different genre, my eyes looked for some love material. *Man, Woman and Child* – No, I was not asking for a child at this stage, I was only pushing for the child's mother. *Every Love Story is a Ghost Story* – Crap! She would only be scared of falling in love. *A Walk to Remember* by Nicholas – not bad! I picked it up and handed it over to her; she excitedly took it in her hands. I had not read it but I lied to her that it was an amazing book with a great story of love. Soon after lying I realized she liked guys who were truthful and I should not have lied. The sun was fast vanishing and it was going to be 6 soon. Her brother would pick her up.

"You better leave now; Hitler can be here any moment," she said with exactly the right amount of sadness that was necessary to make me feel she tried hard to say it.

"Thanks for being such great company," she said.

"I am glad. It was real fun being with you," I replied with a shy smile. More smiles were exchanged for a few seconds.

"Hope to meet you soon," I said in pain.

"Real soon," she blinked and the cell phone in her hand vibrated.

"He is here." It was the time to sneak out. Quite unwillingly I began taking my steps back, slow steps in the beginning to maintain closeness till possible. I felt like going on to say I was in love with her despite being not so truthful. Our hands remained in the air, waiving at each other, and I tried to somehow convey that going away from her was not easy.

That night, I confided in my sister (love can't be clandestine for too long). I told her how I had met someone in the train, how she transformed me, how madly I was in love, of course the last part, hesitatingly. She looked at me with anger in her eyes; that anger was mainly because I had told her about that night quite late. Soon, she had bombarded me with questions like, "How does she look? Tall or short? She should not be fat. Is she? She is fair or dusky? What is the color of her hair? Brown? No black?

"Yellow," I said out of irritation which led to another set of questions. What? Oh my God, is she blonde? She is not Indian? Look I am telling you she would not fit in our family. Their culture and ours are worlds apart." My irritation soared as I began to look here and there, and waited for my chance to utter a word. After minutes of babbling, she became silent and I got my chance to speak.

"See, she is an Indian. Her name is Shreya. She is from Varanasi and she was in my school Sunbeam," I clarified. She raised her eyebrows and bit her tongue.

"So did you say it to her?" she asked.

"Not yet." I replied.

Does she even know that you like her? (She was becoming highly impatient.)

"I am without a clue. But I love her truly," I responded. I had never been so candid with her before. She expressed her surprise over my changed nature. Love changes everything, our nature, our behavior, our soul, everything. She pulled my leg for fun, asked me more and more about her until late at night. I answered all her questions with unabated enthusiasm, later on I realized, I was talking to myself, she had dozed off.

ROCKY IS A MAD MAN

Next morning, I was up early, anticipating the possibility of her call or a message. Despondence hugged me tight when for the next few hours I received no call or message. I consoled myself thinking she must have been occupied with packing but that consolation collapsed soon, her sudden plan would not even have allowed her to unpack. Trying to come out of the bad feeling, I decided to get ready for college. Nitish was going to pick me up in his brand new Alto which was gifted to him by his father on his not so significant achievement; he had somehow managed to get promoted to the final year of college after wasting a year in second year. Only to hate myself later, for a second I was tempted to think that the best thing God can give you is a rich father. He had really worked hard, only I could testify this, no one else could even imagine how he hid important answers in his underwear. Throughout the exams he had worn large size underwear which had sufficient space to accommodate a few sheets. It was such an immaculate trick that despite being frisked in class, he never got caught.

I found it so lousy. I thought I would never do something of this sort to pass any exam on this earth.

"A man's underwear is like the den of a lion. Not for some other reason but because nothing can trespass the two easily," This had been his dialogue and it was stupid and senseless. Complete crap.

On the way to college Nitish told me about our dangerous economics teacher who was on the boil over me as I had not attended any of her lectures for the initial two weeks of the session. He warned me it was important that I showed up in her class to fetch the marks that were at her discretion. I thought in my head that my score had not been so impressive in the first two years so I needed to take things seriously now. I had had a girl in my life lately. So what if she was not my girlfriend; so what she was going far away from me? I loved her like a guy who was off his head and if my love was true which it indeed was, nothing else mattered and I would get her one day. So a beautiful wife, a good job, a decent flat on one down payment and lifetime EMIs, a small car if not big, enough money saved in a bank to afford a yearly trip in the same continent, my dream curtailed to these things. Does this happen in love? Our ambitions take a dive. Sachin Tendulkar would not have reached such a dizzying height, had he fallen in love like this. He would have dreamed only of a flat and a car being in love. Now, I am sure he owns many flats and such luxurious cars. That is the difference love makes to you. You begin to think ordinary. I am sure those mad looking researchers have the same to say.

We reached college. I thought of calling Shreya but again I abstained. It was then I found it hard to beat down the desire of seeing her once, before she left. I glanced at my watch, made a quick calculation and decided to leave after attending the economics lecture which was actually crucial.

Mrs. Kulkarni entered our class. I sat sandwiched between Nitish and Satish. Satish whispered her name into my ears the moment she stepped in. Her appearance made me gulp; she looked calm-headed from nowhere. She took out her attendance register and started taking the attendance without acknowledging our good morning that well. It was my turn now; "present ma'am," I said tentatively. I prayed that she moved to the next name, but that did not happen. Slowly she took off her spectacles as if it was a Ray Ban glare and she was a hero from some south Indian film. I wondered why she had to take off her glasses to look at me; if that helped in seeing better, what was she using it for.

"On your feet," she sort of yelled.

I stood up in a slow motion while everyone turned their heads in my direction.

"So Mister, what brought you here to this stuffy classroom today?" She fired her question quite aggressively and looked at me with real hostile eyes. In silence I swept the grey cemented floor with my eyes as I tried hard to fabricate an excuse to save myself from her. Normally I was good at coming up with instant excuses on such occasions, but at that moment I was dumbfounded.

"Was my question difficult to understand?" she shouted to meet my frightened eyes.

"I was out of the city," I spoke, but she intervened.

"I am aware of this. Your friends told me you were partying hard back in your home town." I looked to my left and then right, Nitish and Satish ignored me. I felt like grabbing their neck between both my elbows. They were the root cause of all this.

"You better change your track by being a little sincere," she advised with least friendliness. I chose to remain quiet; any use of words could have spun her head. It was like if you don't make any movement, the bear would sniff you and walk away. Any movement would get you killed.

"You may sit down," she screamed. Her voice echoed in the whole class.

"Dude, neither of us told her this. Believe me," Nitish and Satish said in unison to which I paid no heed. She began with equilibrium, elasticity and stuff. For the first fifteen minutes, I paid attention then I lost interest, despite the fact that economics had been my favorite subject. Meanwhile, Satish and Nitish discussed accountancy in a soft voice; they were preparing themselves to please a hot fresher by solving her doubts in the subject. They fought over the rules of debit and credit. As far as I could see, both of them were wrong. They did it when Mrs. Kulkarni was busy explaining a diagram on the board. I decided to send a message to Shreya. "Ready to leave?" I typed on my phone and sent it. When I raised my head, Mrs. Kulkarni was looking at me, this time over her glasses. I shivered in my seat. She asked me to stand up again, and again I drew the attention of the entire class. In that precise moment I was preoccupied with so many thoughts. How would I run to see Shreya after the class? How would she feel to see me? Good or bad, I had also thought about debit and credit that Satish and Nitish discussed. I had tried to figure out my own concept of it. It's always debit the receiver and credit the giver. Debit what comes in and credit what goes out, debit all expenses and losses and credit all the gains and incomes.

"What is the law of demand?" She asked as I stood with a blank head.

I was so lost in other things that I did not pay attention to her question. I even forgot I was sitting in economics class.

"Debit the receiver, credit the giver; debit what comes in, credit what goes out; debit all the expenses and losses, credit all the gains and incomes," I said dreamily, totally lost.

"Dude what are you saying? Dude, are you off your head?" Nitish and Satish said in a low voice. Suddenly I gained my coherence, all other thoughts vanquished. But no doubt it was late. Mrs. Kulkarni was looking at me with her big open mouth and eyes; someone had surely given her an electric shock and that someone was me. Upon looking at her, my mouth automatically opened as I realized what I had done. I looked around and almost everyone laughed that worked to shake her where she stood like a statue.

"What debit? What credit? Law of demand is about debit what comes in and credit what goes out?" She yelled like hell. I looked at Satish and Nitish; they looked at me with both pity and shock in their eyes. Shock because even they could not believe what I had done; pity because they well understood that now I was in big trouble.

"I want you to appear in the principal's office after the class. Do you get me?" She said in a freaked out tone.

"Alright, ma'am," I replied faintheartedly. She had been so pissed off that she did not teach after that, she kept on looking at me with fire in her eyes.

The class got over; I was supposed to go to the principal's cabin. Everyone still looked at me.

"Dude, how are you going to handle the principal?" Nitish asked.

"I have heard that diva is mad," Satish said.

"What Diva? Who Diva?" I asked.

"Diva is Deewakar," Nitish said.

"And who is Deewakar?" I was getting mad.

"Our new principal, who else?" Satish explained and I looked at them with irritation. Now came free advice from them by the dozens.

"Dude, say you have problems in your ears and you could not hear Mrs. Kulkarni's question properly." That one came from Nitish.

"No man. Say you ran into a pole and your head got hit badly. And now you are behaving like mad." That one came from Satish.

"I think Satish's idea is stupid. If you are mentally unfit you simply can't explain anything to anyone. They say someone who is mentally disturbed never gets to know about his disturbed frame of mind." Nitish contradicted Satish. Soon they both landed into a debate.

"Guys, just relax. I will handle this," I said, though just to make them quiet, not really because I knew how to handle the situation.

The moment I reached the principal's office, my cell phone beeped with a message from Shreya. "On the way to station", her message read. I needed to hurry now but before that, I had to encounter Mr. Deewakar and Mrs. Kulkarni.

"Sir, may I come in?" I said as I opened the door.

"Hmm," Mr. Deewakar produced the sound.

I went in bashfully to see Mr. Deewakar who was playing with the big globe on his table while Mrs. Kulkarni casually flipped through the pages of a magazine. Mr. deewakar raised his head to look at me and so did Mrs. Kulkarni.

"So what has he done?" Mr. Deewakar asked.

"I asked him a question, What is law of demand? You know what he answered. Debit the receiver, credit the giver. Debit what comes in, credit what goes out. Debit all the expenses and losses, credit all the gains and incomes."

Mr. Deewakar heard her heedfully and his expression turned confused. He stopped the revolving globe with his hand, looked at my face for a few seconds before he spoke.

"Law of demand? You see. Law of demand states the relationship between price of a commodity and its demand. The relation is actually inverse. When price rises, demand falls and when price falls, demand rises," He said as he sank in his big chair. I was puzzled, why is he explaining all this to me? I questioned to myself in my mind.

"Do you understand?" He asked.

"I already knew that, sir," I said.

"Mrs. Kulkarni, he already knew what law of demand is." He turned his face to Mrs. Kulkarni and said it quite casually. Mrs. Kulkarni was totally perplexed and she just threw a look of disbelief.

"Mr. Deewakar, do you think a final year student cannot answer a basic question like this?" she said

"Exactly, Mrs. Kulkarni. That's the point." He was very much convinced.

So? She said.

So what? He said.

"He intended to make fun of me. Do you realize that, Mr. Deewakar?" She raised her voice.

"What? He made fun of you?" He asked astonishingly.

I had almost laughed to break the silence of the funny situation but then I controlled it with a lot of effort. Mrs. Kulkarni held her forehead with her right hand. Next minute she stood up from her chair, she was kind of boiling in that air-conditioned room.

"Mr. Deewakar I must say. This college can never be a disciplined place under you," She fumed and turned to look at me. I avoided her eyes and continued examining the floor.

With her loud footsteps that apparently had to do with her anger, she left the room. Mr. Deewakar looked at me absentmindedly and he began playing with the globe again.

"Young man, do you know what made Mrs. Kulkarni so angry with me?" He asked.

I pulled my lips closer to my teeth to destroy all possibilities of breaking into giggles, saying a word was so difficult. I was sure I would laugh incase I opened my mouth but with great struggle I somehow managed.

"How am I supposed to know why she became so angry, sir?" I said.

"Oh yes, how would you know, my boy!" He nodded as he stopped the moving globe.

"Sir, I need to hurry for the next lecture. Can I take your leave?" Now there was very little time left in departure of Shreya's train.

"Oh yes. Go... go..." he said. As I turned back to storm out of the door I heard his voice again and I had to stop.

"I hope you will not give other students some stuff worth gossip?" He asked. So for the first time until now, he proved that a certain small percentage of his mind actually worked.

The style with which he asked me this made me feel as if I had caught them kissing and now I could spread this news in the whole college. Our principal and our economics teacher are an item, or some such stuff.

"It's not even one percent likely that I will do something so bad, sir," I assured him.

"You are a wonderful boy." He said and again I fought with a smile.

"Thank you for liking me sir." I said and left.

Satish and Nitish had pressed their ears on the door and when I came out they began asking questions. They had seen Mrs. Kulkarni coming out of the cabin first with a completely annoyed face, so they were puzzled.

"Dude, have you been suspended?" Nitish asked.

"What was he doing with you inside there?" Satish asked. I hated his question. I had not gotten assaulted inside; it was surely not the case with me. I was all safe.

"Guys, chill, nothing happened." I said as I told them all that happened inside. They jumped and laughed, I laughed too.

Now was the time to run. That mad principal and that mad economics teacher had already eaten up all my time. Now there was hardly any possibility left of seeing Shreya before she left.

I ran as fast as I could, took an auto rickshaw as bus or Metro was more time consuming. It was a bright day and I was in a frenzy; seldom had I allowed such freakish side hidden in me to come out this way. I requested the auto driver to drive fast and a few times I fought with him when he slowed down or stopped to pee in the bushes which were available to him on one side of the road. The desperation in me had begun to perform salsa and samba. I looked at my watch again and again; I was really not going to miss seeing her. In case that happened, it was going to kill me.

By the time I reached New Delhi railway station, half of my body already hung out of the auto rickshaw. It was a mad jump and I rushed towards the platform. I ran huffing and puffing to reach the platform. My eyes looked for her – left, right, just everywhere. I could feel she was around but I needed to find her. It was not a good idea to ask her about her coach at that time, I knew she was going to feel awkward seeing me but it really did not bother me at that moment. By doing that I was going to mutually convey to her about my feelings, those feelings which were now burning into a flame. I had to run a long distance to reach the AC coaches as they were after the sleeper ones. There was no chance she could be found in a sleeper coach so I had moved to the Air-conditioned coaches. I decided to first check all AC 3 tier coaches as I boarded one coach and walked madly towards its other end. It was full of tourists, white people who spoke some other language, might be German. Without wasting a second I moved into the next two connected AC 3 tier coaches but again it was a dry attempt. So clearly she was in some other AC class, I ran hard, hitting a man who lost his balance completely and fell with his briefcase. Actually his briefcase fell first and then he fell on his briefcase. He yelled and I ignored. I was in AC 2 tier now; my eyes worked unstoppably to trace her. Suddenly my legs stood still and I took a breath of relief, my chase had come to end. How relaxed I had been at that sight! She was right in front of me. I was kind of panting; my eyes flickered speedily out of fatigue. Because of numbness, my mouth could produce no word, nor did I have something to say to her. Hitherto, the curiosity was just to see her. I wanted to speak nothing for hours but only wanted to capture her in my eyes, every movement, every expression of hers, for my relief.

She had been reading the book that I had chosen for her. I noticed she read it attentively as if it were a text book, surely it felt good, that book was picked by me for her. A few seconds passed like that before she took her eyes off the book. At first she gave me a casual look and in a flash when she realized it was me, she was stunned.

"Rohan, I can't believe it!" Her voice echoed for once as she jumped on her feet. By now we had won the attention of passengers around but I wanted to ignore others completely. She walked closer to me, throwing her book back on her seat; her expressions testified her perplexed state. I had no idea of her astonishment; I had been too involved in seeing her face.

"Are you seriously here? God!"

After holding my silence for a minute more I realized it was necessary to say something, if not the truth.

"I was hanging out with friends nearby so this great idea struck that I should say happy journey to you," I said.

"You hang out with your friends at the railway station?" She contradicted almost immediately. I had nothing to say in response; it was the time to allow her to get some signals.

She watched me in disbelief and my disheveled appearance debunked the truth. I noticed that she noticed my straight-from-the-bathroom hair and my breathlessness (result of a bad run). I moved my hand on my hair, hesitatingly, in an effort to style it back to usual.

"Your appearance says you have been running for hours," she said in a heavy tone. She was completely right; I had been running a marathon, only and only for her. But I was not supposed to admit that, no doubt. So I gave her a different reason, knowing that it was stupid but that was not the concern as I had to just say something.

"Well I have started running; it makes one fit and slim. I really do not want to try any Japanese belt later in life to get a flat belly." Her giggles could not be suppressed. Then she checked her watch and told me that it was the time for departure. We both reached at the coach entrance, I got down and she stood at some height on the doorway of the coach. I had not wanted her to climb a running train, not unless I was there to hold out my hand and pull her inside.

"So am I in danger from your brother or driver here?" I asked, just to keep talking.

"Not really. Hitler was busy so I used a taxi. But you felt this fear quite late," she said and smiled. I smiled looking down too, I was safe.

Then I asked her to be very careful as she was travelling alone. She said she was quite used to it. We heard the engine sound, and with a sudden jerk, the train moved.

" By the way, it is great that you hang out with friends at the station," she said in a raised voice to be heard about the sound of the running train.

I smiled, words deserted me again. The train was slowly gaining speed and I had to walk very fast to keep pace with it.

"Hope to see you soon," I kind of shouted.

"May be within a month; details over phone," she replied. And no reply could be better than that, I felt relieved. From that point, I would wait to see her next.

I realized the speed of the train was almost unmatchable so I asked her to take care of herself. She nodded as she waved at me. We kept looking at each other till we could. I continued to look in the same direction for the next few minutes even when there was no view of her. Her last words managed my emotions or I would have gone mad only because she was gone. It was a feeling so inexplicable. It was surely "*Pehla nasha pehla khumar.*"

Days were rolling on faster. It was the time when my days would start with Shreya's thoughts and would end with the same, despite 599 kilometers between us (as claimed by a railway ticket to Varanasi). I was successfully getting close to her, not a single night passed when she missed to call me up for a long and light conversation. My loving sister had become my love advisor. It was because of her advice I had still survived without uttering those three words during our regular conversations over phone. My sister had wanted me to keep things limited to friendship for at least a month; she warned me about the consequences of proposing her so early and how many times I felt like disobeying her. She had disclosed some ridiculous facts about her gender. According to her, most girls, out of apprehensions, on hearing a guy's love declaration, responded with questions and statements like "Isn't this just our third or fourth meeting? What is it exactly that made you fall in love with me? Why me and not some other girl? Do you like me just because I am beautiful? (If the girl is beautiful.) I think it's just infatuation and that's like a disease in all you guys …no no this is not love in actuality. I am just not that type. It's too early. I think I need some more time…" Fear of getting those responses had me convinced to keep it gradual and steady. I was dreaming to spend my entire life with her. It was surely an option to wait for at least a month. My love had only grown in myself. I tried to know everything about her, her likes, dislikes and that only doubled and tripled my love. We both were fond of bathroom dancing; I imagined our future in bathroom, rock and roll.

PYAR MAANGEY PAISA

Soaring expenditure on recharge vouchers had become a matter of great concern for me. By now a huge debt already hovered over my head. There was no friend left who was ready to lend me any more money. In the wake of my impoverished condition, I desperately looked for some source of income. Soon I found a home tuition in Gurgaon through a tutor's bureau. I was required to teach Math to a twelfth standard boy and Social Studies to his sibling in the eighth standard. Their father was a trader in Hong Kong and they were paying really well so I jumped at the job without thinking much. I got to know from their mother that the guy was a spoilt brat who took his studies as a joke; as far as her little daughter was concerned she told me she was totally opposite and used her brain a little more than needed. It was my duty to give her assurance that she need not worry. After revising the whole syllabus of math the previous night, I reached for my first class with them. The class was early in the morning as they had no school that day and I needed to rush for my college lectures after teaching them. They appeared before me without any hi/ hello, not even good morning. Truly they were kids of a rich father, arrogant and haughty, so to bear with them it was important that I kept my own ego at one side. I greeted them which was accompanied by a smile and it was shocking when they did not give me a reply, a smile was surely out of question. For once I reddened like a carrot splashed with water but then I thought about my own purpose, money and only money. My plan was to give a lesson to the girl for reading and begin with the boy before I forgot those large formulas that I had managed to keep in my head for so long. After consuming a few minutes in deciding the chapter I was going to start, when I looked at him, I found him asleep on the chair. It badly got on my nerves but I maintained my cool as I woke him up and asked him to go and splash some water on his face. Then I thought to start a chapter for the little genius, which is what I had heard about her from her mother that she had the tendency to overuse her brain. I explained a chapter on history from her book to her; told her the old name of Surat that was bander-e-soorat and wondered in my head about the rubbish stuff I was teaching her. On knowing this she raised questions like, "what does bander-e-surat mean? Who named it bander-e-surat? Was it a place only for monkeys? Was it a jungle?" It was then that I realized that being a teacher was not less than being the president of the country. I told her the questions she asked were of no relevance and I moved on with other things. Her face clearly said she was unhappy, but in no way I could actually manage to answer her questions. Meanwhile the boy got back to his seat and I felt a certain kind of smell all of a sudden, it was a light smell that comes out from someone who has just thrown the one inch debris of a cigarette after smoke. I looked around and wondered from where it came. All windows were closed so there could be no one out in the balcony with a cigarette. I looked at the boy and now I was very sure that he could be the only source of that mild smell which had begun to lose its little effect by now. So I struck a conversation with him using facial gestures while the girl was busy reading her chapter again. It was something of this sort with no words involved.

Me- Hmm,

Him- What?

Me- What kind of smell is it?

Him- No idea.

Me- It's of a cigarette.

Him- Oh!

Me- Did you just smoke?

Him- No.

Me- But this smell?

Him- Do you smoke?

Now I could not stop myself from going mad, I had had just about all I could tolerate.

"Look. Do not even try to act up because you don't have the faintest idea of my temper. I tell you. You can't dance on my head." I gave him a thrash of words and ignored that he had actually smoked.

For the next half hour, I taught them almost nothing, the

guy pretended to memorize the formulas and the girl asked me a few more stupid questions that I ignored.

Despite my bad experience with my students I still felt satisfied thinking about the money. But that satisfaction could not enjoy a long life as soon something happened that made me dizzy. Their mother called me that evening and said that the little genius was not satisfied with me as I ignored her questions; in short she meant I was fired. Then she went on to say something that was frustratingly embarrassing for me. She said a teacher should never smoke just before teaching his students. When I heard this, my mouth automatically opened like that of a crocodile. The only difference was that a crocodile makes a big mouth for its prey and in my case I was the prey myself with a wide mouth. I felt the loss of two things – money and respect, and those two things are the most important things for anyone.

Nitish's brother was running a consultancy that offered jobs in international call centers. It was going to be my last hope, but even working in a call center was full of troubles for me as my father had some kind of enmity with call centers. He had this weird thing in his mind that it was just because of call centers that India was producing a falling number of doctors, engineers, scientists, etc. According to him, an increasing number of youngsters were sidetracking their career towards BPOs instead of going for the elite courses. But I had no choice left, I desperately needed to work for at least a month; money had become a big hurdle now. I decided to tough out by joining a call center without adding anything to my father's knowledge. I would really have no bold answer if he asked why I needed money.

My good speaking ability got me a job in an international call centre, though on fake documents as they hired no college goers. I was assured of my first month's salary which was fifteen thousand bucks, I was told that it was pretty safe as any kind of verification was likely to happen only after a few months and I needed to be on this job only for the first month of paid training. The next headache was my college; not college really but attendance, so for attendance I got a fake medical certificate from a doctor who often made these certificates for Satish and Nitish. My one month paid training began. I simply waited for a month to get over. Beseeching friends for financial support time and again was getting tougher and tougher.

After a week of training that went smoothly, killing time had become as difficult as taking a bath on a winter morning. But my penurious condition, and the fact that money was a must have especially when you are in love, I kept pretending to pay attention to all the credit card details that the trainer explained. The trainer, Sandy, was a cantankerous soul. He had this thing somewhere in his mind that I was a sham; I was least interested in working. Apparently, he took me as a soft target, putting all the focus on me, demanding answers of stupid questions from me, and my happiness was completely screwed up. I was least interested in knowing how we needed to help an Australian in case his credit card was eaten up by his dog. I was not there to talk about credit cards; I didn't even have one. I was there to bring life to my own debit card. Besides I hated Australians for two reasons, one was of course racism (I was following the whole matter on news channels; how Indian doctors, engineers and students were getting killed and facing threats); the second reason was their cricketers, how badly they behaved on the field. I was so thankful to that one Sikh cricketer who taught them a few lessons.

The only solace I obtained which made me forget all the bad things was the time when I would talk to Shreya during wee hours. For her I would do just about everything, I would even help Australians if they had difficulty in deciding the best food for pets, so that there was hardly a case of a dog swallowing a credit card.

My training had crawled into its last week. On my fingertips I counted three more days of imprisonment. As usual, during lunch break I called her. That is when she stunned me by the news that she was coming to Delhi next week. She had to do some shopping for her cousin's engagement back in Varanasi. I praised God, my happiness at that moment was unfathomable. I knew at the end of the week I would part with my financial crisis on taking my salary and in addition to that Shreya was coming at the most appropriate time. Now no more worries for soft drinks or burgers, no worries for recharge vouchers, no more begging from friends. Now very soon I would be a man with a wallet full of notes. I felt kingly, just too royal. But for the second time my happiness couldn't last long. That day when I went back into my training bay and as I seated close to the mammoth table, Sandy entered with an expression that was very grave and on his bad face it looked even graver. He broke his silence only to pose a threat to my heart. The words from his mouth shook my head from inside and my whole body quivered, I had been horrified like never before.

In a voice which had the touch of anger and devastation, he said, "After verification it has been found that among us there are two people who have not been genuine with their documents."

For me it was a typical Bollywood movie scene where the heroine is newly married and someone tells her that her husband (the hero) is dead fighting enemies or villains. There is a loud nahiiii, and then she breaks her red colored bangles on either a table or the wall. In my imagination, I screamed a big no. I had not put on any bangle on my hands else I would have surely banged my hands on that big table. It was yet another failure, this time it was much more painful. I knew I had been caught, all my dreams collapsed, I had not expected something like this at all especially when it was all going to get over so well. My head bent down, my lips pressed, reluctant to hear a word more, Sandy continued in his low tone, "It is upsetting that I have received an order to call for a couple of terminations right away." I closed my eyes, took a deep breath to hear him take my name. "Sakshi and Varun, both of you will have to leave immediately."

I took a few seconds to realize in that posture, that I was neither Sakshi nor Varun. I was Rohan. I opened my eyes suddenly, raised my spinning head, and looked around with my traumatized eyes. Varun and Sakshi left the room in silence.

Nobody had ever thought that there could be something fake about them. After they left the room with Sandy I normalized myself and prayed to God, so that I was bestowed with two more days of safe-breath. I was least interested in seeing that place again once I had much-needed fifteen thousand rupees in my hand as my salary.

The shift and day got over, I boarded my cab and my mind cogitated without a pause. I was still in the foil of anxiety and negativity. I called Varun to know more about the situation and he told me that he had shown some extra months of fake experience to fetch a higher salary, and that he knew nothing about any kind of verification possibility. Fear seized me; I imagined the possibility of my turn the next day. Before sleeping that night, I prayed over and over and asked God for fifteen thousand, though I knew it was going to be highly improbable. By now they would have discovered that I had fooled them.

The next morning when Sandy entered the training bay, I almost fainted with the smell of impending danger; danger that could have left me with empty pocket in love . I only breathed when Sandy began his voice training session. Somewhere deep down I thought maybe I wasn't yet caught. But every time he called my name, my heart skipped a beat. Minute by minute, second by second, the day passed and I felt I got really close to my hard earned money. Sorry for the use of the phrase hard earned as it was not, I admit, but if you see through my self-centered angle, you would understand why it was hard earned for me. God was surely showering his blessings on me, my reality was still under tight wraps. That day everyone talked about Varun and Sakshi, I had to become a part of the talk too. I thought in case I get caught, the next day I would be the butt of all talks. In the last two hours of the shift, tension built up to an unbearably high level in me. But nothing happened that day too, I was still alive with my hope.

The following day was going to be the final day, the day when I would insert my Citibank ATM card in the cash machine and take the cash. That night after dinner when I was on my bed, planning how to allocate the amount I was going to get, something more than frightful happened. My phone beeped, it was Sandy who called. The first thought of my mind had been "Have I been caught? Is he calling me to say Rohan you are fired?" In all those deadly thoughts, his call ended. My throat had been far away from the condition to utter a word. I anticipated that I was gone and so was my money. Falling in love in this modern world is an excessively costly deal. But once you are trapped, there is no escape; you lose the ownership over your heart and you bear the cost in the literal sense. We often hear men do not cry, during that minute the least that I could have done was crying for hours like a baby. How ill-fated I was, I thought. They had caught me at such a time. I felt a stabbing pain in my heart, now again I would have to worry for burgers and soft drinks while going out with Shreya, again I would have to make sure to haggle with autorickshaw drivers without shreya seeing it. Love had made me realize the importance of money.

It dawned on me that it was better to finish it all on phone rather than facing humiliation publicly. Besides I knew Sandy was going to take all his frustration out on me for the trouble I had caused him during the training; this was going to be his opportunity to level attacks. I called him back with my tremulous fingers. I said "Hello Sandy" in a shaky voice.

"Yeah Rohan, I just need to inform you … I hope you can spare a few minutes to talk…" I knew what he had for me. Talk, go ahead, you bastard, tell me that you people have caught me and I wasn't needed to show my face.

I said "Yeah tell me…"

"Tomorrow being the last day of our training, we are planning a small party after the shift so in case you are interested you can join us!" He said. I sighed with relief, patted on my heart, everything was fine. I couldn't believe it. I lied to him that I was very much interested, the call was over. I felt extremely happy and relieved.

The next day during the first session of training, I was more than excited. On inquiring from some people, I came to know that there were two more hours left for our salary to show up in our accounts. Every time Sandy went out and stepped in, my heart sank. Two hours seemed like two complete ages. I had still not received the money but I felt like a thief who puts all costly stuff in his bag and is on the verge of running away. My legs had been at unrest out of fear and excitement. Two hours passed, when I came out of the training bay during the five minute-breather, I ran (this time like a bull out of its mind). I reached the cash machine, inserted my card and straightaway checked the available balance. My account had still been empty. Now I had to spend some more time at that place. An hour passed, I decided to take one more chance. Again I sneaked out of the training room when Sandy was off for a few minutes. I entered my pin number, fixing my eyes on the screen, and suddenly my eyes lit up. The screen flashed fifteen thousand as available balance. I would have danced inside but I noticed there were a lot of eyes on me from people who stood outside in a queue. I withdrew all the money immediately and made a quick count, there was no chance of any error. I had fifteen thousand rupees in my hand. On stepping out of the Citibank cash machine, I stretched my arms and the happiness on my face was not ready to fade. Now there was no need to go back to that loathsome training so I scampered off. I took a bus back rejecting Sandy's call over and over. Shreya, the boy is rich now!

BOYFRIEND NAHI, TROLLEY SAHI

The next week Shreya reached Delhi. I had waited for her the way a prisoner waits for his release order. Her stay was going to be for four days this time and she had already informed me that she would be wholly occupied with shopping for her cousin's engagement ceremony back in Varanasi, but still she said that we would meet.

That evening I asked my sister whether the time had come or not. She replied by saying "You figure out yourself, you know better about what she feels for you." I hated her when she said it. It was because of her that I had controlled my galloping love and now she was asking me to figure out myself whether it was the right time or not.

"I don't know but yeah I am sure she likes me. We spend hours on phone, but I don't know if this means something," I said. I wished I could tell her that waiting for a day more was like swimming across an ocean.

On seeing me disconsolate, she giggled and said, "You are behaving as if you have already proposed to her and she has broken your heart into a zillion pieces." I looked up to her face. "Go ahead my brother, express your love for her." she said in a tone that encouraged me. I felt elated. Now I just waited to meet her.

The next morning Shreya called me up; she sounded low. Nobody was free to give her company and that had spoiled her shopping mood. The girl of my life was sad like a kid. Fatty and chatty were busy with some exam preparation. It was not actually bad that they were busy. This was my chance, a wonderful chance, an opportunity to say it to her.

"I can carry your shopping bags." I said tentatively. The texture of her voice suddenly got better.

"As in you can..?" She asked.

"As in of course I can. Free for the day."

"Great... great... great..."

"But..."

"No buts, please."

"But I mean it... I can only carry your bags like a trolley. I am a terrible shopper."

"Oh trolley is cool," she laughed.

"Fine then, cool..." I said and clenched my fist for everything was falling in the right place.

"Come on rocky, get your baby," I spoke to myself.

We decided to meet after two hours at a Metro station. I thought about my plan to propose to her and it made me nervous, so damn nervous, as if I was going for a math exam without any preparation. My body shivered as if there was a generator running inside me. I had fallen for her every second and now I had to express it all, I had to give words to my feelings. There was no time to plan, so I gave all the responsibility to my heart. She reached five minutes after me. Stunning as ever, ravishing as ever. My eyes caught her from far away as she flowed towards me. I began losing my senses once again. We exchanged "Hi". We chatted while we climbed metro stairs, on to the platform. We talked with better energy and I realized we shared a relation already. She told me innumerable things, about her mother who was diagnosed of some liver malfunction, about her cousin who was getting engaged. I wished she talked about me who was getting mad for her. We boarded the Metro train.

"Hey, just look around," she said as the door of the train closed after us.

I looked around and paid attention. Wooowoooo. I found girls everywhere. Shreya was not aware of the new Metro protocol of first coach reservation for ladies, so it was purely my mistake. I held her hand and moved to the next connected coach. It was the first time I held her hand and that happened by mistake.

"Oh! Sorry," I said as I left her hand jerkily.

"So, how often do you do that?" she asked.

"Often, what? I just held your hand for the first time," I said, not understanding her reference.

"Oh! Not my hand. How often do you board a coach full of ladies?" she asked and laughed.

"Not until today," I replied and smiled.

We reached Connaught Place where she bought no clothes, but just accessories. I noticed she was poor in the art of bargaining. She paid by the price tag for every single item she bought from the streetsellers and I thought I really needed to earn a lot of money for a girl like her. Connaught place failed to hold her interest for even a second more than half an hour and now she wanted to quench the rest of her shopping thirst in Dilli Haat. One, two, three, four, five, six, I made a count of poly-bags, six already. The trolley could still accommodate a few more. We reached Dilli Haat in an auto rickshaw. This time I did not look for a chance to fight with the driver for ten bucks or least five, rather I paid with open heart. Dilli Haat was a new place to me and it was a place exclusively for girls. As Shreya tried different shades of bangles on her hand, I waited for the right minute to unveil my love for her. We moved from one shop to the other, bangles then handbags, handbags then footwear. I wondered she needed so many things just for her cousin's engagement ceremony. When she asked for my help, I helped her judiciously with full interest. Wherever my mother was at that moment she would be unhappy as her son barely helped her in shopping. Love makes you do what you actually don't like doing. She shopped with unabated enthusiasm, I just stared at her and it was a reverie. Polybag count was ten and now she complained of painful legs after she got tired. We sat down under the shade of a tree on wooden chairs. I realized she must have been thirsty so I brought two bottles of coke along with some chips. As I saw her taking huge gulps I imagined the possibilities of her reaction when I would tell her that I loved her. What if it gave her a big shock? What if she said we were good as friends? What would I do? How would I live? I would be shattered because forgetting her would be like impossible. I could not summon enough temerity to say those words to her no matter how noisily my heart shouted. After a full bottle she got back her energy and got up for a few more things that were left. I followed her with my thoughts running tirelessly. In half an hour more, she was done with a lot of poly bags on us. And soon we left. We sat silently in the auto rikshaw as she was all worn out and I was lost, though I kept looking at her in the front side mirror. Many a times I tried to open my mouth but I was rather apprehensive. We stopped at some distance from her house and she went off giving me a smile.

On reaching home, I straightway rushed into my sister's room and told her all that happened, told her I could not say it. She heard me with a smile and after a few seconds her smile faded as she felt I was distraught.

"Let's just find out what she feels for you," she said.

I liked her sudden idea but I asked, "How?"

In confusion I saw her doing something on her phone and I tried to get a clue of what she was trying to do. My phone beeped and I took it out in hurry as it could have been from Shreya. I got obfuscated to see it was from Di who sat right in front of me. She laughed and said, "You thought it was Shreya? You have gone nuts, I tell you my brother." I continued reading her message. It was the one meant for lovers.

"What is this for?" I asked.

"No doubt, you are daffy. Just forward this message to Shreya," she commanded.

"This is crazy," I protested.

"Let's see what her reaction is, this can give us a hint," she explained, I mulled over for a few seconds and then I sent it.

I didn't have to wait for long as I received a reply from Shreya in a jiffy. It read, "Lovely message thanks".

She further ordered me to type "Just for you!" I protested again but she forced me, so I followed her order.

This time she replied "Uhhh.. han.. I see, I am glad!" My face got ignited as I showed that message to my sister.

"Boy, this birdie is freaking out in love," she said. Further, I could not stop myself from giving her an enveloping hug for what she had done to help me. There was surely something in Shreya's heart for me too after the slight investigation that was conducted by my great sister. Now one more chance and rocky would not hesitate in saying I LOVE YOU to the baby. To know about the possibility of a meeting, I called her and she upset me with the news that her sister-in-law had taken leave from her teaching job for two days and now they would go for some more shopping. So now they planned together two full days of shopping before she boarded a train on the third day. I asked her a risky question, out of high desperation, about how much shopping she was left with. The items in her list were still many in number. Before the start of anything, she had already scared me with her shopping appetite. But then

I loved her, so I needed to love her shopaholic nature as well. Anyways for a second I thought to say it on the phone. But I had read somewhere that love proposals on phone are not very successful. I had already got a chance and I let that chance go easily. Only a good idea could favor my love. I extracted one at two in the night but it demanded creation of a whole set up, but I knew exactly what was needed to be done. Guys, she was again travelling alone to Varanasi.

I phoned Saurabh at that unearthly hour.

"Man. what on earth made you call me at this time?"

"It's damn urgent!" I said and tried to sound very serious to beat down his sleep.

His voice got active soon and he said, "Tell me".

"I am travelling to Varanasi soon and since I lack an excuse, you are dying in a hospital after a serious accident." I narrated the plan to him. Now he was not required to die from an accident but just participate in my plan.

"Hmm ok no problem.... you could have told me all this after sunrise, now can I sleep?"

"Wait and listen," I cut him off.

"There is a problem; dad might talk to your mom for offering condolences," I said.

"Hang on; I am not dying in real."

"You will if you don't deal with this problem for me."

"Fuck my ass. Man that does not sound like a big problem. We have dealt with such cases before." He said in confidence and I demanded him to elaborate.

"Did you forget Rita from my dad's office who had saved me once by talking to the principal over the phone and calling herself my mother? She will help us in this," he said. Of course I remembered it quite well even after years that once my friend was caught kissing a young girl who was a sweeper in our school. He had taken a chance on all the girls of the class and at the end he notched up a girl with broom in her hand. Our principal was over the boiling point and Rita had helped him in saving his life. So Saurabh was finally allowed to sleep.

My mind started giving finishing touches to our plan. Next morning, I called up Shreya to know about the train in which she had a seat booked as I had to make sure that I booked a ticket for myself in the same train. An agent got a seat booked for me in the same train by charging a lot extra over and above the actual fare. So now I could board the same train with her.

At last I had to go through the most challenging task of handling my father which was also the most complicated task. To avoid nervousness ruin my plan, I called him while he was out for work. Words suddenly vanished from my mouth when I heard his "Hello!" I summoned enough audacity and opened my mouth to inform him that Saurabh had met with a serious accident, giving him all the gory details that he had several major fractures in legs and arms as it was significant to create an impact. Something like forty stitches, two major fractures, four minor fractures and missing movements in certain parts. I also tried hard to sound all teary and on the verge of breaking down. In the end I expressed my willingness to go and see him. As I waited for a backlash, he sounded like he was convinced. He hung up after he said, "Check if you get a reservation." Out of delight, it had almost slipped off my tongue that my reservation was already done but thank god I managed to hold my tongue.

Now I desperately waited for another very special journey with someone really very special. There was no question arising in telling Shreya about it so she remained oblivious of my hidden plan. The hands of the clock appeared motionless again. Everything had looked perfect until something happened that washed away all the possibilities of another journey with Shreya. Her father arrived in Delhi from nowhere to attend a seminar and to spoil my plan increasingly. He was now taking her by air along with him, a day before her intended train journey. When she told me this quite heedlessly, I went speechless. My exceptional idea of expressing love in a moving train certainly got grounded. So far I had made it look very possible, but her father's unexpected entry into the whole scene demanded the use of the words pack up, and there was nothing practically possible to take the act ahead.

Now there was hardly any point in waiting anymore, through whatever way but I really needed to talk. Showing boldness and candidness was the only option in the situation. I called her before being sure of what to say but when I heard her voice, I began prattling in a dull tone.

"Shreya, can you possibly manage to meet me before you leave?" I heard nothing in response, and without bothering I moved on to say, "Now that you will leave with your father, my plan will go waste." I talked like a jerk.

"Plan, what plan?" She demanded explanation and due to some recently felt openness, I chose to speak. I told her everything; about the reservation that I got for myself, about my plan to surprise her. I knew I was indirectly signaling something to her rather expressing but I was not going to stop this time. She heard me meticulously and when she finally spoke, all my sadness vanished.

"Can't we still do something?" she asked. There was eagerness in her voice too. Her use of WE purported a variety of things. It was surely a dhinkachika moment. I could not believe what I had heard; with such little efforts from my side something had become very clear. She was craving for me too; she was waiting for me too, like I was craving for her, like I was waiting for her. To believe this, I had more reasons now.

"Still do what?" I stammered and preferred to act dumb. "Still do what" was not that difficult to understand but I simply decided to offer her the driver's seat and preferred taking the back seat myself, hearing more and more from her is what I wanted.

"Do what you planned doing Rohan…"

"Oh yes, and by doing what?"

"Maybe I can plan out something?"

"Please plan to save my plan."

Her plan one was a no go, plan two for a second offered the ray of hope but missing flight would necessarily lead to her father boarding train with her next day, plan three was the safest but not really the simplest.

"Hey! This might work. I can give an excuse to my father that Shruti is accompanying me this time and if I cancelled then it would not be good." She spelled out her plan number three; I felt the girl was quite instinctively brainy.

"This sounds good!" I managed to say, tried not to sound too excited. Had I showed my excitement to her, her excitement would have taken a dive.

"Too good."

"Just great."

"Ok now let me try this, can't do late. I will call you back," she said.

"Good luck!" I whispered.

The matter was closed right then, rocky thought he got the baby. The fact that she was going to lie to her father for me felt simply marvelous. She called me again after an hour; my heart beats went out of check, too strong and noisy, as if I had a heart of an elephant inside me.

"Rohan I have managed to convince dad but then there is still a problem."

"Don't tell me your dad will come along?" I asked impetuously.

"No, of course not."

"Thank god. Let me guess then. One you will have no Shruti, two you will have me. Three I can't be Shruti." I said in jest.

"At times your humor sucks, I tell you," she said like a girlfriend says to her boyfriend.

"No. Is it? Really?" I asked but I knew such non serious remarks by a girl are positive indicators always; a girl says like that only to her cute boy.

"Oh Yes. Now listen to this. It's most likely that Hitler will come to see me off at the station, if he comes then we need Shruti." For a second I took it as a problem before my razor sharp brain produced an easy solution of the problem.

"Has he seen Shruti before or ever met her?" I asked inquiringly.

"Nah! I don't think so," She replied instantly.

"Be specific!"

"No I am sure he hasn't."

"Then there is no trouble. My dear sister can play Shruti in this whole act," I laughed.

"What? Your sister? No way. What would she think?" She said with a show of slight anxiety.

"Just breathe out all worries, she is sister cool," I calmed her.

"But this will be so embarrassing," she objected for the last time because then I chose to tell her that my sister had been hearing her name for the last so many days. It silenced her and I knew she was enjoying the silence. She raised a few more questions and I gave a few more answers. Now everything was fixed, there was hardly any more obstruction. I had combated it all rather we had combated it all with perfection. For one last time, I checked if there was still a boulder on the road to be pushed aside, here is the mental check list.

Dad- Check

Her dad- Check

Rita (to act on phone as Saurabh's mother in case required)-check.

My sister- No check needed. Everyone should get a sister like her.

Her brother- Check (with my sister playing Shruti)

She- Check twice.

Me- Check a thousand times.

Now I just had to think about those beautiful moments that were going to come. I took one complete day to finalize a gift for her. Initially I bought a wooden Taj Mahal for her but when I showed it to my sister, she gave me a dirty look. Old fashioned, orthodox, such words she used to describe it. So I gave it to Sudy (Sudish); I would not use the word servant for him, he was like a part of our family. Recently he had started going out with Rupwati (maid from next door). I would make it clear, together they would go out every morning to dump the garbage at the nearby garbage dumping station. So ultimately that Taj Mahal fell into Rupwati's hands. He gave that wooden Taj Mahal to her and promised that one day he would build a real one for her. Then I realized it was a real stupid choice of gift by me. Taj Mahal is not alone a symbol of love; it also signifies that no matter how much you do for the person you love, it can't overshadow the Taj Mahal of course. It's like at max that I can try for Shreya is a bungalow with a garden or a 4bhk flat with car parking. Taj Mahal was out even of my dreams; even an ordinary Mahal with less magnificence would take away both my kidneys. Finally I bought a silver bracelet for her and got satisfactory comments on it from my sister. God! Rocky is hell of a lover, let him win.

HUT, HILL & THE OCEAN

I gulped from my bottle of Pepsi while my sister and her friend Priya chattered animatedly. Priya joined in to offer company to her friend. Shreya informed me on text message that they were reaching shortly, so the girls with me decided to get into action after seeing my lady love.

The train of my life waited for yet another interesting journey. It was a fantastic atmosphere at the station, cheerfulness and joyfulness everywhere if seen through my eyes. Our eyes remained fixed for a glance of Shreya, the girls with me were getting barmy to have a look at the girl who was coming. The three of us stood near the coach that had a seat for me, this time our seats were not in the same coach.

"Call me up as soon as you reach," my sister ordered with a big smile on her face.

Suddenly my eyes caught sight of Shreya as she moved down the stairs towards the platform. I made the two girls with me notice her immediately. I heard my sister say to her friend Priya, "This dumbo has got a doll yar." My chest size doubled on that but next moment I interrupted at being called dumbo. Not to forget, she walked towards the train with an abnormally tall person who was supposed to be her brother. It was time for lights-camera-action. We rushed inside the train with a small bag that had a pair of shirts and jeans for two days' stay. Now we had to wait for Shreya's call.

"I can get keyed up. I am not professionally sound for this task. Can't act. I will simply laugh over there," Di said as she put down the weapons being a soldier in the situation.

"Come on, it's not mountain climbing. Just forget your real name for some time, and yeah, you can't laugh," I said after tasting the heat myself.

At that exact moment my phone vibrated; that made the three of us look at each other. I picked.

"Shruti I have reached," Shreya did as had been decided.

Now was the time for Shruti (my sister) to go to Shreya and her brother, do a bit of acting and leave. Di left us and I prayed she did her job well without being nervous. Time had passed drastically to our wonder; I checked my watch and got uneasy when I learned we really had very little time left. Priya and I waited until I thought I was a stranger to Shreya's brother and could have been near them without risk. Priya got down from the train as I asked her and I got into Shreya's coach. I walked carefully like a passenger who was looking for his seat. Shreya and Di noticed me. They all were talking cheerfully to each other and then I got down. I took out my phone to remind Di it was the time for her to leave.

At this point Di was required to leave saying she was going to get her bag. In the nick of time, she came running and I gave her a one side hug for her flawless performance. A thank you was too small on the occasion. She had been exemplary as a sister; I was overwhelmed for what she had done. I ordered them to leave that very second; she gave me a few quick instructions again and I heard them cautiously. They left. Di kept looking back at me, waving, motioning me to board the train. The screen of my cell phone flashed 'Shreya Calling'.

"Where are you, Mister?" She asked as if she was getting mad to see me, I admittedly felt delectable.

I had wanted to say "Sweetheart give me a jiffy!" though in reality I chopped off the word 'Sweetheart', she could have taken offense at that; officially we were not yet a couple. Now it was pointless to anticipate any more hurdles, we had gone through many already. No doubt I still had to say that I loved her. But my confidence had surely improved, I boarded the train, looked into the dirty mirror, I don't know how that smile appeared on my face just on seeing myself in the mirror. I felt tingles running inside me as I headed towards Shreya. When we both saw each other, we smiled. She sat with her legs up on her side lower seat. My place was reserved right in front of her as she had already made a successful request to its occupant to give it to us and accept a seat in a different coach. I sat in style, suppressing all the hesitation in me. There was noise yet there was silence; we gave a chance to our eyes to interact. The more I looked into her eyes, the more I fell in love with her. I sighed with my eyes on her, she burst into laughter.

"You look tired after fooling people," she said. I laughed heartily for the first time with her. We felt an abrupt jerk, there began the journey of love, the train moved. After a long 'eye to eye' session, we began to exchange words. A couple of hours or three passed without a clue. We talked about several things, books, movies, many more things about our school days. Love was still not discussed. When we rested our mouth for a few seconds, I thought about the idea of proposing to her. After a bit of thinking, I reached the conclusion that the air conditioned coach was not very ideal for the situation. There wasn't any strong breeze, no visible sky; the beauty of nature was missing. All that was a must at the time of proposing to her. The thought of proposing in a packed surrounding was too deprived of vogue. Again I had to put stress on my already stressed brain to make it all very unique.

I plunged and asked, "Aren't you feeling the absence of fresh air?"

She was startled at the question, "Yes but we don't have a choice."

"Of course, we do," I responded. My tone was too optimistic. I stood up to complete the mission, she was bamboozled. I entered into the connected sleeper coaches and ran my eyes; I had looked for a seat that suited us the most. I noticed a side lower seat; a middle aged woman who was most probably travelling alone lay on it. Around her were mostly old people busy in their own worlds. They are the kind of passengers who sleep early in train, mostly keep their eyes closed in search of peace. I stumbled towards her; I had been great in the job of handling aunties. My friends would be amazed to see how easily I convinced their mothers for the night outs and the birthday parties. She looked confused to see me approaching her.

"Ma'am can I make you a request?"

She replied in affirmative, though with reluctance.

"Actually my friend is down with fever and we happen to be in AC, she is shivering. Would you mind taking our seat in AC so that we could…?

She interrupted with a big "Yes!" It looked like I announced that she had won a prize worth millions. I smiled, the job was done. I went back to Shreya, told her it was done. I lifted her two heavy briefcases, she offered help and I refused; girls admire strong men I, knew it. We settled on our new seat. Dusk was showing signs of taking over the day, Shreya looked out of the window and she was full of excitement.

I seated meticulously, "So, do you like it here?"

"It's amazing here" she replied. The weather outside was beautiful, the air that touched us was fresh and fragrant. Now everything was the way I had wanted. We were quiet again. I was lost in her thoughts. I don't know what ran in her mind at that time. Every time our eyes met, something happened, I felt a spark. I could say she felt the same. We talked in soft, measured words. It was dinner time and when I was ordering food, she said she carried sufficient food for both. We planned for a late dinner. Soon everyone around us became tall and flat on their seats, even the lights were given rest in the night.

"Are we going to have dinner tomorrow morning?" she joked. In all darkness, she took out a box and two plastic plates. Two plates were not needed I had thought. As soon as she opened the box, its smell suggested it contained something that was my favorite. She placed two scrumptious *aloo paranthas*. It was a dinner like never before. I couldn't believe it was all real and I was not dreaming. After dinner we both went to the washbasin together, I saw us together in the mirror, what a couple? I said to myself. Shreya got frenzied to see the moon that had lately emerged. The radiance and glimmer of the moon added to the beauty of the night. Shreya's face looked incredibly beautiful in the white light. The next moment she asked me whether I could sing and before I could come up with an answer she reminded me of the occasion when I had sung in school once. How could I have said no to her? I thought she made it easy for me; it was an easy opportunity to express it all in the form of a song. The song that immediately came to my heart was one of Enrique's famous hits. It was 'Hero'. She turned silent as she waited for me to start. Without any nervousness, I started.

"Would you dance, if I ask you to dance?

Would you run and never look back?

Would you cry if you saw me crying?

Would you save my song tonight?

I can be your Hero baby!

I can kiss away the pain,

I can stand by you forever,

You can take my breath away…"

Silence followed, our eyes clung, and soon my breath got powerful. My song had caught her heart and soul; it was evident from the way she looked at me. Now was the time when I could not have resisted the uproar of my feelings.

"Hey, I badly need to admit something," I began.

"I am listening," she said in a soft voice.

"I have never felt like this before."

"Felt like what?"

"I wish you could know how I feel these days," I was failing to word my feelings.

"Of course I know because I feel the same way," she said.

"Really, you feel the same?" I asked her quite frantically.

"Yes, but the way you said it, I felt like you had a stomach upset and I was your doctor," she said with a smile.

"Sorry I could not do better. But I just love you."

"And only that matters. I love you too," she replied in a few seconds.

As soon as I heard those words, I went blank. It was like a strong wave that calmed suddenly. I wanted to shout, I wanted to dance and I wanted to do all those mad things. I took her hands into mine. She looked at me admiringly.

"I love you Shreya."

"I love you Rohan."

I gave her the bracelet and asked her to try it, she liked my choice. I sat next to her now. We kept sitting like that for hours, with our fingers interlocked. I told her it was like a dream. She had pinched me so as to make me feel that it was all real. I laughed, she laughed too. We talked the whole night.

When it was close to dawn, I found her asleep with her head on my shoulder. I made sure to make no movement. I saw her face. In the presence of very little light, she still looked radiant. Her eyebrows were actually in the shape of a hut, her nose was tall like a hill, and her eyes were not less than any ocean.

BACK IN VARANASI

The next morning, we reached. Our houses were in the same locality and her house was pretty much at a walking distance from mine. At home I spent some time with my grandmother. Heard about her joint pains, new curtains, the old refrigerator that now gave new troubles, about the marriage of Duggal uncle's daughter Panny, also about the milkman who had made a habit of supplying milk with more water. From so many things which she told me, only her joint pain enjoyed my attention and rest I was in some other world. My happiness was at its peak, we had planned to meet up at 2 in a mall. Varanasi had recently seen the opening of a couple of shopping malls. I lied to my grandmother that I was going to meet some school friends (now that she is no more I seek her forgiveness for all my lies, but I am sure of getting it for our deep love that we shared, rather share). I was supposed to meet her at two and I jumped on the driver's seat of the car quite early at one for a fifteen minutes' drive. The desire to be with her was towering. I drove straight to a flower shop, Shreya loved roses and it is also a notion that a guy must give roses to his girl if he actually loved her. Some twenty fresh roses I bought, one was not sufficient. I reached early, parked the car in the basement, adjusted the rearview mirror such a way that I could see my face and then adjusted my eyes in the rearview to give a final nod to my face that had already got enough face cream used on it. Men can't avoid touching face creams at times. I took a lift and made an entry into the mall. Shreya arrived soon, she was wearing jeans of a light shade and a blue top that looked great on her. She looked unbelievably pretty. I wanted to take her in my arms but it could have been too reckless, hugging culture is not so popular in Varanasi as in Delhi. Here the way love birds meet, they give a feeling that they are brother and sister, and they are there to celebrate Rakshabandhan. A small city has many people with narrow minds, so it's safer to go the brother sister way. Delhi is decades ahead in certain things I must say. Here lovers meet differently. From far away they exchange flying kisses, on meeting they hold hands or the guy holds the girl's waist as a gesture of love or whatever you call it, then they sit so close to each other as if ready to make out in public. So we both seated like brother and sister in a coffee shop.

The first question I asked her was, "How much time does this poor fellow gets with the queen?" Before she could respond, I said, "I mean the maximum."

She laughed, pouted her lips and did a bit of calculation.

"Comfortably two hours," she said.

"Then? Are you comfort loving?" I asked with a smile. She smiled too.

We had pretty decent time and in a snap I was ready with an idea of how to spend those hours with her.

"So just get cracking," I stood up and demanded her to leave her seat using my hands.

She was left in bewilderment; she questioned, "Where?"

"Time is running out. We got to leave," she jumped on her feet after making a cute face. I felt like kissing her crazily. Inside the lift, we talked through eyes. When we reached the parking, I opened the door of the car for her quite gently, she grinned and I loved it. I ignited the key and with a stroke we moved. After covering some distance, I stopped the car. It was the time to give her those roses that I had kept below my seat. I wore a somber expression to make her believe that there was something wrong, something worth worrying. I succeeded as I noticed signs of anxiety on her face.

"I guess one of the four wheels is punctured," I mumbled.

"I will check my side you do the same on your side," I somewhat ordered in a serious tone. She obeyed as she put her head out through the window of the Maruti Zen. After she observed the wheels and found them alright, she turned back and was stunned to see so many roses in my hands. I could confidently say she was totally enthralled. She took the roses in her hands, ran her fingers on the petals, it seemed that she loved them.

"You surprise me all the time," she said with a shy smile. I looked at her in admiration. After ten minutes of drive we reached our school where we had spent years without knowing each other. We went inside. The school canteen was the first place we decided to visit together and then we planned to go to the auditorium where all school events used to take place. Inside she told me where she had seen me first, near one water cooler. Now that was heart touching, she remembered it .Then she reminded me of a very funny incident that happened when I had participated in a Marathi folk dance, the guys had to wear a *lungi* and it so happened that the knot of my lungi got undone, it made me run offstage in the middle of the performance. Then I told her how she had cried on stage during one poetry recitation competition. She laughed and admitted it was stage fright. I joked I had planned to flaunt my hot legs taking off that lungi and that it was no mishap but an act of skin show. On the big stage she forced me to perform a few steps of the same Marathi dance that had remained in my mind as nothing more than an ordeal because my lungi had almost come off. At first I kept saying I remembered not even a single step of that stupid dance but she was adamant and forced me to perform something stupid. I began to recall a few steps. From hundreds of empty seats Shreya occupied one in the front row and became the only member of the audience to watch my electrifying performance. I climbed the stairs of the stage and reached over to the center.

"Chill… no flying of *lungi* today," She said after covering her mouth with both hands to be audible to me in that large auditorium. Then she laughed, I replied with a smile.

"Come on, my hero," her voice echoed. I performed clumsily yet confidently for a minute and when I stopped,

Shreya stood up and clapped for something that deserved only a mad laughter. But then she cracked into laughter. I almost jumped from a reasonably high stage to cover those few meters between us while she continued laughing with a red face. Together we laughed, then hugged after we laughed, finally kissed after we hugged. That kiss was mainly the outcome of an initiative from my side and an acceptance from hers. I took my head closer to her with a certain kind of intention, she welcomed me with her eyes, and I kissed her. After a body numbing kiss, we rushed out. She kept repeating all the way back how great she felt and how much she had enjoyed herself. I dropped her a few blocks away from her home and waited as she walked glancing back at me now and then. Five minutes later, she called me when I was driving back home. She had left her wallet in the dashboard of the car, so she needed me to drive back which was more of a chance for me to see her again. I took her wallet out and kept it on the next seat. The next time my eyes fell on it, I noticed a photograph which was peeking from inside. I thought it had to be a photo of Shreya or of her mom or dad, I couldn't control myself from looking at it and with my left hand I picked it up. I opened it between my hands on the steering wheel. I saw the photograph, my heartbeats nearly stopped. I forced my right leg on the brake as I felt a big jolt in my heart. That photograph definitely had Shreya who smiled, but with a guy. I looked at the photograph again which was making a hole in my heart, my fingers trembled. My phone beeped again with Shreya's call, somehow I picked but my voice went missing.

"You coming na?" she asked, all I could manage to say was "Almost there." I drove as fast as I could. Within a minute, I reached. She got inside, there was no contact between our eyes. I had failed to hide my miserable eyes, she burst into laughter. I turned my head towards her in amazement and my expression was a combination of sadness and astonishment.

"Just a cousin," she said nonchalantly.

"What?" I said and watched her with confused eyes, with no clue of what was happening, mystification unabated in me.

"That guy in the pic is my cousin; that wallet was gifted by him with that pic in it," she explained. I continued being wordless, her w ords gave me stupendous relief. I had felt as if I just used an oxygen mask and now I was able to breathe for life.

I still had nothing to say, "I am sorry, I just…" I spoke in an abashed voice.

"Now can I have my wallet?" she smiled.

"O ya," I said as I handed over her wallet shakily.

"And learn to drive slowly," she sort of threatened. That had felt good, her threat. She got out of the car abruptly.

"I love you," my voice echoed. I read her lip movement that said "I love you too." I drove back home laughing at myself.

Late night I called Shreya and got to know that she was shivering with cold. It made me tense as our plan to meet the next day was now uncertain.

Next day, the day I was supposed to return, it must have been very early in the morning when I called her to know about her fever. I knew it would not be possible to meet her even once that day if she still had fever. Her voice had not been so great; I felt sure of no chance whatsoever of seeing her before I left. She sounded weak. I desperately wanted to see her; after all it was for her I was there. That visit of mine had been so eccentric and distinct, normally I would call friends, organize a gang up, go to Ghats, do parties, but this time it was all so different. After a flurry of serendipities, it was time for some unfavorable things to happen. I would have to return without seeing her, it spoiled everything. She sounded sad and upset as she blamed herself for it. Then she asked me to meet my friends and I refused to do that initially but when she forced me, I agreed. I took a shower, without a song or a Michael Jackson move, perhaps a melancholic song of late 70s or 80s. Saurabh was not in town so I called Siddharth. Just for the sake of Shreya I drove mournfully to Siddharth's house in my unhappy mood. He consistently and boastfully talked of his girlfriends, how frequently he changed them almost like clothes. It only got on my nerves. I was a guy in true love and hearing all that was slightly or more disturbing. I left him quite shortly as I thought being alone was better. It was an unusually not so bright day in Varanasi, with the sun hiding in the clouds. I left Siddharth's place, drove back home monotonously. I called her sitting in the car with the hope that she might be feeling better and we could meet.

"Rohan, aren't you with your friends?" she asked surprisingly. I had tried to figure out whether she was still laid up with fever.

"No, I am not." My voice was far away from being lively and energetic.

"Why, what happened?"

"Nothing I went to meet Siddharth, I didn't feel like staying there for too long. I am sitting in car right now." I expressed my grief, I believed the texture of my tone had conveyed her that I just wanted to see her and nothing was more significant. But nothing seemed to get better. She was still not fit enough to come out.

"I know you are missing me and so am I," she said in a sad voice.

"Hmmm."

"Wait, can you just hold on for 2-3 minutes."

"Yeah fine, I am here," I said as I dismally rested on the seat. She put me on hold for quite longer than the time she asked.

"I am so sorry, am so sorry, am so sorry," she was back with casual apologies.

"Hey that's okay."

"Do you want to see me?" She asked in her beautiful tone. I was puzzled, with my lethargy certainly vanishing, how could I have said how madly I wanted to see her. It was the only remedy to my peculiar woes.

"Yes, but…" I mumbled.

"So come on look into your rearview mirror." She commanded cheerfully. I jumped on my seat, glanced into the rearview frantically, Shreya had been right there at some distance on a pink scooty. I was wildly excited. It was almost getting impossible to overcome my bafflement. She said in a serious tone after a short laugh, "Hey you have seen me enough, now let me go." My eyes were fixed on her directly, without the help of rearview.

"Hang on, no," I screamed in my packed car.

"Rohan, please."

"Please, no."

She couldn't hear those two desperate words as she had already hung up. I saw her going back, going far from me, a sudden energy hit me and I ignited the key. I made the car take a U-turn, gear turning to fourth in a flash, my right leg going hard on the accelerator. A couple of minutes later, I drove parallel to her scooty. She looked at me with enormous surprise; I looked at her with enormous intensity. She screamed "you are mad" a few times.

"Left" I shouted. By taking right she would get to her home, so we both headed towards the solemn cantonment area which is a low density place full of nature. I turned on the music, songs of Enrique again, volume set extra loud.

"You are mad." She said as I drove next to her scooty. The emptiness of the road allowed us to enjoy all that was happening. She kept giving me a girl's shy looks, I watched her with my eyes feeling high relief. We reached a place that was quite safe, I motioned her to stop and I got out of the car. She parked her scooty as she faced me. I walked close to her and when we offered our hands to each other, I felt the temperature she was running.

"God! You shouldn't have come out," I said.

"You sure I shouldn't have come out?" She smiled and replied.

"Can't say I am sure or not," I took a step more and she was in my arms. In seconds I felt her hands at my back, she held me tightly as we felt lost in each other's arms. A car passed only to disturb us and we had to leave each other. We smiled.

"Hey, no one knows I am out in this fever. So I should be home now," she said.

"Yeah, let's move and I love you," I said the last three words with a different seriousness. This time she took a step ahead and as she kept her head against my chest she gave herself into my arms. The moment took me by great surprise; I held her and made myself feel that I owned her.

"I love you," she whispered. I kissed her forehead, quite a hard one, not willing to take back my lips.

I realized we were ignoring the time somehow and so we moved. We both left together. When she entered the big black gate of her house I drove along the boundary wall for a few minutes and left. I felt much happier now as suddenly it was all superb. The way she came out for me, the way she hugged, the way I felt with her, it was all like a dream. Love was at its peak.

NO BACHCHAN, NO TENDULKAR,
BANJA ACCOUNTANT

I was back in Delhi, though, my heart was still in Varanasi. A few days passed. Shreya had again remained unsuccessful in making it to any of the medical institutes. This happened very much in her favor as her interest lay in a different field. But even this did not offer a better hope because her father had already lined up a college for her in Dehradun after she showed no success. I struggled to respond when she told me unhappily that she was finally taking admission in a college. She was clearly upset over her father's decision but Dehradun was not so far away from Delhi, so this time I did not tell her to confront her father. That long distance in our long distance relationship would shorten and what better could I expect. Besides, Dehradun is a less costly city and spending four weekends every month was not going to cost a bomb at that place. So I thought it was simply great. One evening when I told my sister about it, she made me realize how important it was for me to do well in my own career. Quite confidently I told her my plan of doing masters in business administration and quite brutally she laughed at my plan. At first she raised a few questions over my potential of cracking something as tough as CAT. She judged me as someone capable of any other institute but not the IIMs. Then she thought if Shreya's father was so particular about making her a doctor then he would be equally serious about getting a highly successful son in law. A highly successful son in law, it sounded poppycock but in any case I had to become someone highly qualified in order to come up to his expectation. My easy plan of going for an MBA degree the next year suddenly appeared so trivial to me. My sister felt there was no match at all, a doctor and an ordinary MBA. Here it was more devastating because the girl was a doctor and the guy an ordinary MBA. No matter it was not her choice to be a doctor but now it was almost certain. The question I faced was disturbingly knotty: could I really do better in my career for the girl I loved. A career in films was full of struggle, politics sounded equally hogwash, and one peculiar thought suggested that I make crores by solving the problems of the people through television. News channels those days had created headlines with news of a Baba who had made some two hundred crores doing this. That baba gave me high inspiration for a minute as I thought it really did not matter whether I was a doctor or engineer with two hundred crores in my bank account. But then a Baba so young would never appear to be potent to those who lack either wealth or good health. Besides, which father would give his daughter to a deceitful Baba. The only option left was chartered accountancy. I realized it was not so appalling, plus it matched with the course I was pursuing. The course was reputed and the prospects it offered for future were also bright. So I was ready, dreaming up a giant firm in my own name with big clients who would be good payers. No doubt I was late by not less than two complete years for the course but my sister cleared the hesitation. Even Shreya was quite late in getting a college so I could start and notch up too. So now once again I had a complicated task to perform and it was to persuade my father for chartered accountancy. When I told my father that I wanted to do CA, he gave me a dirty look.

"What is suddenly so interesting in CA now?" He asked in his all time strict voice. I obviously had no logical answer for any of his questions. So reliance was all on rubbish answers.

"I just realize my duty of doing what you feel I should," I said quite hesitatingly and melodramatically.

"Go straight to your point," he asked.

"It's for you I have decided this," I replied trying to sound confident.

"Oh this is highly surprising," he laughed as I blanked out.

"You don't feel it's really very late now," he said after he finished laughing.

"Yes, but not late enough." I showed a good quality confidence that made him silent.

But when he spoke again, it only bred more difficulties for me.

"Look son, actually I have realized my fault, I know it's because of me you have changed your mind but I am totally with you now. How can I be such a ruthless father who doesn't give his son the freedom to do what he wants?" I felt giddy, too irksome; I knew God was playing games with me. I remained wordless for a few seconds and looked at my father without any ideas. I lacked patience to fabricate something fresh now.

"It's not just because of you, but I think it is the best for me," I said less dramatically this time.

"It's because of me and then the next moment it's not. Hope you are not drunk."

"You know I don't drink," I lied as the task got complicated. While we were in the middle of a hot discussion, his cell phone rang and it seemed to be from someone important from the style of his talking. It really gave me some time to fix my sanity and composure that was needed to win over the situation. He spent some good time talking on the phone with no attention on me and it only irritated me like hell. Once he removed his phone from his ear, he threw a look at me which was full of surprise. More ignorance came my way for next five minutes before he finally spoke.

"What can I say? If you are very sure then go ahead. After all, that was my first wish," he said. I heaved a sigh of relief. Now doing all that was not less than getting a Taj Mahal built for your love. When I had informed Shreya about my changing plans, she had been quite convinced. But after a few days when we talked about it again, she sounded different.

"Is this all for me?" she asked.

"Yeah I thought I needed to be good career-wise. I don't want your parents to have any objection in future, when you tell them about me." I spelled it out for the second time and wondered why she demanded this explanation after being totally convinced that it was important for me to shape up my career well.

"This is simply stupid, you can't decide on everything keeping me in mind," she sounded raucous. Her voice sounded bitter than it actually was.

"What do you mean, Shreya? Are you trying to say you don't see your future with me?" I asked in an aggressive voice.

"Look Rohan, all I mean is, it's better if we are practical. Life is full of twists and turns." I heard her gingerly. Her arguments and words appeared impalpable to me. I talked of love, and she talked of being practical. Lately, I had discovered that love is never practical. It's mad, it's emotional, and it's irrational. You make so many plans for your life, all out of emotions, all from the heart. That night, I kept awake until very late. I thought about her words over and over. Pain had slowly and gradually poured in my heart, I tried to extract something positive out of the words she spoke to me but I couldn't ignore the fact that, she didn't exactly feel the same way for me. The thought was painful and disheartening. Despite all that happened, my love hardly languished; rather it got more vivacious. I chose not to feel too broken, our love was still very new and I was determined to win her heart wholly, I registered myself for the course of CA. Shreya stayed on in Varanasi and was supposed to join her college in Dehradun in a few weeks. I told everything to my sister, how Shreya felt about my career related decisions. She was not very happy to hear this.

DIL TOD GAI AB DAARU LAO

A couple of weeks went by. I thought I was doing well. At times, through our conversation, I would feel that I had succeeded in being an important part of her life. I made sure that hundreds of kilometers between us took no toll on our love. Long distance relationship is full of foibles and follies, quite true. It happened despite all my genuine efforts, something that I had feared since the day she had seemed different. One morning, I received a text message from Shreya that read. "Can you do something if I ask you?" I read it with perplexity. Though she asked it simply but I was sure that it was not going to be something so simple; she had never asked me for anything before. "Have you any doubt?" I made a text reply. Some ten minutes passed and it was quite a lot of time to understand that there was something definitely wrong. Exactly when I decided to give her a call, her message shot into my text inbox. I read those words with my eyes almost popping out. Those words were "It's over. Forget me". Too callous, too coarse, too concise. A very unusual silence was everywhere around me and I immediately felt the change that occurred only with her sudden absence in my life. But then I wanted to hear some answers, why she was asking me to forget her and what was suddenly so wrong. I gave her a call and she did not accept, next ten or so attempts had the same result. Was she just gone, had she left me completely? If yes then why? No one could love her even one percent of what I did. So why did she throw me out of her life like I mattered not even a bit? I called her again, quite recklessly this time, but I did not hear a word from her. She did not take the call. That silence was still looming as I walked lifelessly towards the window of my room. The sky looked exactly the same; the traffic on the road was busy like every day, nothing was still except my life. She had severed it in a style that gave rise to many doubts in my mind. If I took coaching from my mind it said she was a sham, she was treacherous, but my heart was contradicting my mind. The way she had come into my life, which was far beyond my strongest imagination, she walked away exactly in the same way. Leaving it all for a joke, my love, my fate, my faith, everything. Soon that silence changed into aggression and I decided to leave for Varanasi. I made myself conscious of the time; there was the chance of catching a train that left in two hours. In ten minutes I got ready for the next train journey which was going to be very unpleasant. I went to my sister and told her about it and that I was going to Varanasi to meet her. Initially she tried to change my mind but it did not work, I was determined to meet her. At New Delhi station, I stood amid hundreds of people, totally flustered. As the train arrived I stumbled towards the general class (I was going to travel without prior reservation). Boarding a general coach was really not easy as these are terribly choked with passengers. But I had no option. Unlike others, I stood peacefully at one side and waited for a smooth boarding. After a few minutes, I stole a chance of boarding. As expected I barely had enough space even to stand as there were people even on the floor. A man who sat on a piece of cloth near the wash basin accommodated me. I was grateful to him despite the bad smell that he offered. All the memories of those two nights spent with Shreya in train had come alive once again.

The next day when I got down the train, I felt terribly weak as I had not eaten anything for more than a day. Straightaway I took an auto rickshaw for Tagore town (Shreya's place); I was clueless of my actions. The morning was flawless, cool breeze, mild sunshine, but nothing appeared pleasant to me. I reached Tagore town, paid for the auto rickshaw and moved recklessly towards Shreya's house. It was an excessively insane move I was making, but nothing could stop me at that moment. Finally I stood in front of Shreya's house. I tried her phone and it went unanswered. She had severed all things with me and was not going to answer my call. While I walked around to figure out her room, I noticed one open window and on looking with more curious eyes I saw flower pots that were placed in a row. Shreya had great liking for flowers, something that I knew, so I thought this was the right window and hoped to see her. A few minutes passed, in one moment, I saw her as she passed from one end of the room to the other. I opened my mouth but stopped myself from saying a word as it was not the right thing to do at that time. I still looked at her window and I really had no answer for what I expected. The moment came soon and she now stood at the window with the kind of expression on her face that actually gave me the pain that was by no chance less than the pain caused by a hundred injections given at one time. I simply watched her, with no idea of what I was going to do now. After looking at me in disbelief, she disappeared. I raised my hand to stop her but did not succeed. Before I could think of anything, my phone buzzed and it was Shreya. I picked but hardly got a chance to utter a word.

"This madness is not going to get you anything," she said, her tone, unusually acrimonious. Her words fuelled my pain, what a bad feeling it is if you get such things to hear from someone whom you love deeply. I was experiencing all of this in love; it was the turn of feeling the pain.

"But I love you Shreya." I said laconically. My throat had not allowed my mouth to utter too many words. She paid no heed to my words.

"Go away please, everyone is in here."

"No, I won't go anywhere," I said aggressively this time.

"Fine, meet up at burger king, 2' clock." She hung up. I stood there for a few more minutes before walking away from her house. My phone vibrated again, it was my sister's call this time. For minutes I tried to answer all her nagging questions quite apathetically and then unwillingly heard everything that she said in order to make me understand. She also asked me to call Saurabh who knew everything by now, she had already phoned him. As soon as I finished giving her fake assurances that I was going to handle the situation sensibly, Saurabh stopped his car near me. A bear hug that I did not enjoy even a bit knowing he was in the habit of taking bath once in a fortnight, a sad look that he gave me quite deliberately and then he began moving towards Shreya's house which was only a few meters away. I was not going to stop him from doing what he was planning to do. Only by giving a high amount of stress to my eyes I believed that my insane friend had actually dared to press the doorbell of her house. Just at that second when he did something so lethal, I screamed to ask him if he had freaked out. My loud voice shook him so badly that he began running towards me and the car, like a mad fellow. We dived into the car, he made us move in reverse gear for some long five minutes and now we were out of danger.

"Are you drunk or what?" I snapped.

"Man, I just could not control myself after seeing your bad condition," he said.

"And what was your plan to do to improve my condition?" I asked him a bit mockingly.

"I just wanted to convey your true feelings to her," he said casually and his words silenced me, I was no more mystified at his madness and now I thought of a way in which this could be done but nothing could bring Shreya back to me. He kept looking at me over and over, I hardly felt awkward. There was a bottle of water in his car and I splashed some water on to my face, we reached. Inside I found Saurabh's mother sitting on the sofa and I tried hard to sound normal while I greeted her. In her eyes I had always been a mild-mannered boy, without much affectation. I sat next to her for a few minutes to answer her general questions on family and career before I moved into

Saurabh's room. The round clock on the wall, which looked so monotonous or maybe it was mainly my own monotony, showed 10. So still there were four long hours in meeting her and despite all worst feelings I was no less eager to be with her. While I was on the bed I crashed and that happened because of the sleepless night I had spent in train. At 1.30 when I opened my eyes in absentmindedness I first wondered at my whereabouts and then I realized I was badly late. Suddenly the bathroom door made a noise and my vulgar friend emerged from inside in his underwear, he looked scary.

"Man you are up. Feeling better now?" He asked as he took his ugly frame near the mirror. Now that was disgusting, very disgusting, there was a hole in his underwear right at the hip.

"Fuck. Man. Just look at your underwear," I said as I took my eyes off him.

"Dam there is a hole. Sorry man but we are men here. Chill!" he said. Generally, among guys it's the usual thing, I really can't say if it is common among females too. I remember that moment when I was in my school washroom where I got bullied by a few senior boys because I was not comfortable changing clothes in front of them during one school event. They had really hurt me with their comment on me, my manliness was questioned. It had hurt me for days. I still feel uneasy in a situation where I share my room with some guy who is a nudist. Anyways I smelled bad so I moved into the bathroom for a shower. After a not so enjoyable shower I leaped into a pair of shirt and jeans that did not fit me at all, I felt like a fat man. From a plate full of sandwiches, I had one and fought with the second and then I finally gave up. We reached where I was supposed to meet Shreya. I asked Saurabh to stay in the car and I went to the restaurant. My heart grew uneasy; I thought what I would do in case she did not turn up. I occupied one corner table and refused the waiter for an order. She arrived ten minutes late; I stood up the moment I saw her. She chose to keep a plain expression even after noticing me and she walked towards my table giving me the impression that she hardly knew me. As she stopped at a distance of one meter from me, I observed her face which had a clear signal that she was there to hurt me some more.

"I can't be with you anymore," she began to give me more shocks straightaway.

"What went so wrong? Trust me. We can sort this out. Whatever it may be," I stuttered.

"I never loved you. Just never," she said.

"That can't be true," I replied in a low voice.

"I have someone else in my life now. You would not demand any more explanation I believe." Now I felt as if those were not words but boulders hitting my face. She went on to repeat all she said with more coarseness that was killing me, my silence deepened.

"Overcome it fast, it will be better for you. Bye." In the next ten seconds she was gone. I was stunned. A bracelet lay on the table; it was the same bracelet which I had gifted to her in the train.

"Man. Are you alright? What happened inside?" Saurabh asked me quite frantically. Still, I wore the cloak of silence, his questions got no response. We moved out of the restaurant. I was surely into deep thinking; I thought I was a mere toy in her hands. Not even by mistake she was in love with the toy. In the car Saurabh asked me what had happened and I told him the whole story. After hearing everything he went speechless, shocked at what had happened.

He drove in silence. Breaking all silence my phone beeped, my sister was surely fretting like anything. The first question she asked me was regarding Shreya and I told her that it was all over, she had never been in love with me. She became silent for a few seconds and then asked me a not so suitable question. She asked me if I was alright. Definitely I gave her a positive answer but what I felt inside me did not synchronize with my answer at all. She told me she had already transferred some cash into my account so that I could buy an air ticket to Delhi. After I finished talking, I asked Saurabh to drive towards the ghats. On the way to ghats, Saurabh made several efforts to cheer me up, but all his efforts went in vain. I had seen my new life in Shreya who just gave me inexplicable pain. We sat in numbness at one ghat. I had always maintained my friendship with these ghats, the surrounding, and the silence they offered. My head was dizzy, my heart was too uneasy. It was the kind of pain that was driving me mad. Saurabh lit up a cigarette, though I was sinking in a flood of pain. Cigarettes had never fascinated me till that day, I always avoided it. A sudden desire arose in me and I asked Saurabh for a cigarette.

His expression was of a shell shocked man. For years he had forced me to be his smoking companion but not even once had I tried it. But anyways he had no cigarette left in his cigarette packet so he offered me the one he was smoking. Not so comfortably I took it in my mouth and further sucked mouthful of smoke, after which I released it slowly.

"Dude I got dumped too," Saurabh said.

"What?" I asked.

"Yeah she just left me."

"What went wrong?" I asked disinterestedly.

"Last week I took her to a Chinese restaurant for lunch." He said and stopped. For a second I thought if that was the reason why he got dumped.

"My car tank got empty on the way and I simply asked her to give a push up to the nearby fuel station. But she just left in a taxi."

"What?" I said as I sounded louder and better.

He gave a sigh as he said, "I think she didn't like that". I couldn't stop myself from laughing, after a long time. He joined me in the laughter, we laughed noisily, freakishly.

Just before sunset, we reached home. No one was in, his mom and dad had left a few hours ago to attend an outstation wedding. I sank into the sofa before anything else; he brought some food from the kitchen and I made myself understand that my condition was worsening due to my badly fallen appetite. Weakness was showing on me terribly, I was starving. I ate slowly for the necessary bit of vigor, after which I closed my eyes and relaxed. Admittedly, thoughts of Shreya were not completely missing.

My peaceful sleep on the couch was broken by Saurabh; he woke me up in fatherly or grandfatherly style. He told me it was nine at night and that he had a surprise for me.

"What surprise?" I asked, almost inaudibly. Nothing would surprise me, I knew quite well but still I asked him without any heart.

"Just say hi to your sister. She has been worried about you like anything," he said as he pressed a few buttons on his mobile phone and handed it to me. I tried clearing my throat and summoned enough strength in my vocal cords to sound better.

"Saurabh?" she spoke unsteadily.

"No it's me R…"

"How do you feel now?" Again she asked me the same question I hated most in that time. The girl whom I loved madly had left me in dumps. So I was supposed to feel worst and I was feeling more than worst, indescribably worst.

"I am okay," I replied halfheartedly.

"Don't lie. I know you are not." She chose to yell this time.

"You actually have no feeling for us. Your world is over right?" There were signs of tears as well in her voice. As I heard her with intensity, I felt the emergence of a new pain in my heart. It was the pain of being ignorant of those who loved me, cared for me, to whom I mattered. For a moment I thought of saying sorry but I stopped myself, when your mistakes are big, use of sorry only makes you shallower. I kept the phone down, my eyes, not willing to make any movement. No doubt, this conversation on phone made me hate myself like never before. I sat with my face covered with my hands. Luckily I had someone for my respite, Saurabh, the all time happy soul. "Today we drink and damn all these beautiful girls". He was there with his surprise.

I heard silently, but his echoing words made my attention level go better with a rocketing speed. I gave him a look full of bewilderment. But what I saw made my eyeballs dance. He stood tight, in a pose too like Rajnikanth, with a red crate full of kingfisher beer bottles. I had never seen so many bottles of booze before.

"What the F…" I began, shaking off all my anguish.

"Dude aren't we both heartbroken?" he asked with mad loudness.

"Yes we are. So?" I replied.

"Haven't we been dumped terribly by girls whom we loved like hell?" Here he had a point, he loved his girlfriend so much like hell that she left him.

I replied again, "Yes!" In affirmation of my feelings and in suspicion of his, no doubt.

"So like every other man who is left with an ailing heart in love, we can't keep ourselves from the only cure of the disease. This is the time to drink and free our hearts from all despair."

I watched him with all energy now. It was the best comedy he had produced ever with innocence and spontaneity. In a flash, he grabbed a bottle out of the red crate; opened the seal with his mouth, and offered it to me. My breath quickened as I hesitated, I had still considered myself a teetotaler, except for those very few occasions when I came into the influence of my friends. I slowly moved my hand and grabbed the bottle. He removed the cap of another bottle with his mouth, in style, I am sure he thought, doing that made him Bond. We sank into the big couch, with our legs thrown on the table. I started with a small gulp, then a big one, after that real big and long gulp. It was a perfect example of aggressive drinking that you drink when you are unhappy with life, without any hope. When I finished one full bottle, water had emerged in my eyes. I breathed like an animal, heavy and fast. Saurabh gave me those "dude, are you insane" looks. But you barely give a damn to anything in this world when you fall in love with alcohol". I ignored him and reached over for another bottle, one bottle was just not enough for the different kind of disorder inside me. I felt lighter after one bottle and I needed more. Saurabh also joined me by taking some big gulps. After finishing half of my second bottle, I spoke, "Hey Saurabh. I don't know what is going on in my life. I mean so much pain…She crushed it all in a twinkling and walked away. I had put all my love in her," I laughed in an unusual way. It was the kind of laughter that you laugh at your sorrows and pains.

"Dude don't lose hope, life will get better… I am sure. It's like the more pain we get, the stronger we become for life ahead. Don't worry man, don't worry."

I looked at him in great bafflement for what he had just said. "Does he really have a philosophical side?" I ruminated for a few seconds. It could be possible that he improved as a person whenever he drank, at least I could say this. The effect of beer got stronger, I held my bottle no. 3 in hand, and Saurabh finished his second. The next moment Saurabh stood on his feet, quite unsteadily.

"Man, let's goof on the roof now, and get some fresh air."

I had to put in a lot of effort to get on my feet. My head spun, I felt dizzy, my balance crashed and the empty bottle in my hand fell on the floor.

"O shit!" Saurabh said and almost jumped from where he stood to save his friend from falling. That bottle made a cracking sound, and it broke into many pieces on the floor. We both laughed hysterically as we realized it was the part of the show.

On the roof, we sat on the highest place near the water tank, totally sloshed. There were a few countable stars that gave us company. I was 3 bottles down and now I carried no bottle so both of us drank from the same bottle. From the top of the 3 storey building, almost the whole city was visible; Varanasi is not a very big city. We sat solemnly and enjoyed the freshness in the air. My mind was put to rest by the effect of beer, but my heart was still not failing to produce sad thoughts. Not a single night had passed since my mother's demise that I didn't think of her. Her thoughts approached me only in the silence of nights. I had never shared this with anyone. But after you are drunk, you intend to take everything out that is inside, just everything. Emotions roared in me.

"Dude I am missing Ma," my sadness spoke. Saurabh opened his eyes on me; inadvertently I was digging his deeper side if it was actually there. Again, he had a highly intricate job of soothing his friend.

"Hey hey Rohan listen, look I'll tell you something and it's true. One who dies turns into a star and shines in the sky." He spoke with great attempt to convince me. I heard him and this time I was sure it was from a movie.

"Man, just don't be sad. She can be that star." He pointed towards one sparkling star in the sky. I knew he was baby treating me, but I felt better. I considered my mother a real star, and in the clutches of 3 bottles of beer, I believed him. I observed that star with my eyes full of curiosity, but it didn't satiate. I stood on my legs with the support of the water tank next me. My eyes were still fixed on that star. If it was my mother, I was really getting her after long. I spread my arms wide apart and screamed at the highest pitch possible.

"Ma, I love you." I thought it shone brighter. I did the same thing again, and this time tears trickled down my cheeks. Saurabh made me sit down. I broke down uncontrollably. I spoke to myself, audible enough for Saurabh. "Why isn't she replying?" I cried till I was breathless.

The next day, I boarded a flight for Delhi. Life once again appeared fuzzy, with clouds of sadness hovering.

TWO MONTHS LATER

I BECAME A HOT BAR DANCER, NOT ACTOR

The song *pehla nasha pehla khumar* was no more heart touching. I had moved on to the tracks of singers like Jagjit Singh and Pankaj Udhas. Among English singers Brad Paisley became my favorite, love songs were highly irritating all of a sudden. It is true that the feeling of being dumped is the worst of all feelings. I would stand in front of the mirror and wonder if I was really so bad, if I was really not worth someone's love.

At times when I would see a guy holding his girlfriend's hand, I would feel an urge to stop him and say "Dude don't fall in love, she will dump you one day." On second thought I would envy those guys with girlfriends. My sister had given a hint to my friends about my melancholic life and they were ready to fight my pain in their own way. They would drag me to discotheques and pubs where they would perform some Madhuri Dixit moves together; they would also dance around me, making me feel like a hot bar dancer.

Saurabh also tried hard to make me feel that this world was not yet over for me. Once he called me after doing an internet search on 'What helps after you get dumped in love,' his search result said, one should watch porn, read dirty magazines, watch cartoons, play table tennis, wear colorful underwear and of course consume a lot of alcohol. In no case I was going to do all that crap as I enjoyed playing cricket not tennis. I never watched cartoons even when I was a kid. I preferred wearing only black and grey underwear, once I had read dirty magazines that Saurabh gave me but I didn't read them ever again. I never watched porn as I believed it would ruin a virgin's view on sex. As far as drinking was concerned I could go for occasional shots beer.

My sister too was not lagging behind in playing her role of a caring sister and she would drag me with her whenever she went shopping. She would seek my help in choosing her nail paint, slippers, bags, etc.; she would do this to keep my loneliness at bay, but frankly speaking she only made me mad. Soon even I realized that being busy was the only solution and I began participating in college activities. Satish and Nitish buzzed at the right time with some kind of acting hunt in our college. It was for the lead role and few other roles in a movie based on Delhi University students. Both my friends had already begun to dream of stardom, affluence and fame. I thought it would give me the much needed change as I was clearly agonizing.

Now I was a novice in the field of acting, always wondered how anyone could adopt different moods and emotions over the naturally occurring disposition. Clearly, I did not fit in this format of art. Satish had once played Ravan in his society during Navratri whereas Nitish was given the role of a dilapidated scooter when he was in school (of course it was without any dialogue). However the worst was mine: in school my teachers thought I did the best being a tree as I was quite stiff and so in an annual event they made me a tree with leaves and fruits all over my bare body. The feeling was awful but it wasn't as abhorrent as the fruits used on my decoration were all mine.

It was the day of audition and our hearts had been turbulent. The whole selection procedure comprised of three stages. In the preliminary stage, Nitish was asked to play the role of a drunkard, Satish and I got the roles of a mentally unsound man and a reporter. We mugged up our dialogues, practised it many times to ensure a good performance. Nitish went in first, we peeped into the audition room through the window. When he started his performance he looked far from a drunkard, actually he looked like a man with a disability. He walked with twisted legs, made both the eye to look at his nose and raised his left upper lip. He was clearly over doing it as he looked like a handicapped person and not an actor. His twisted legs were a sign of polio, moved eyeballs made him an eye patient, and of course raised upper lip was a result of paralysis.

"Dude I think our friend missed those two drops of life." Satish joked and I giggled. Nitish's horrendous performance was on; the whole crew of selectors fought with a smile while our friend made a mockery of himself quite badly. I wish we had an option to pull him out of the audition room while he was in the middle of his performance. He reached very close to the cameraman despite plenty of space given to him. I am sure that happened only because he had rolled both his eyes to watch his nose, he could see nothing. Suddenly we saw something that stunned both of us. With his next movement Nitish was over the cameraman, Satish and I pressed our lips and caught our heads. Satish was the next one to go in for audition, he was already trembling after Nitish's disastrous performance. He went in halfheartedly and now Nitish joined me at the window. He asked me innocently if I had liked his performance and that made me speechless. I felt like banging my head on the wall. In case I decided not to cause any injury to myself I would catch his collar and shake him.

Satish stood in the centre and this time the man holding the camera stood far away in fear of another attack on him by some mad guy. He uttered the first line of his dialogue, then stopped; Nitish and I were perplexed. Soon he turned and now his back faced the camera, we had no clue what was happening. The selectors were already breathing fire, so they commented, "Dude, we like your curves now show us some acting if you can." Satish made a turn facing the camera, after that comment on him but he still looked oddly nervous to the maximum.

"Come on," I whispered to myself.

"Dude if I can do it you can do too." Nitish said softly. I looked at him with boiling eyes. We looked back at Satish. Satish repeated his freakishness as the casting team once again witnessed his curves, going by their last comment on him.

"FUCK". We said in unison. Now this was the final madness, Satish ran out of the audition room like a rat running away from a cat. I gave him a look that screamed "Dude what the fuck was that?" Next was my turn. The selectors looked exasperated and one of the guys from the crew asked me if I was sure I could do this. I nodded in fear. The role of a reporter wasn't a difficult one for me as I had always paid attention to the way reporters did their jobs on TV. I held a mike to be able to step into the shoes of a reporter. I started off well but then what my friends had done at the same place came to my mind. Somehow I managed to carry on and even managed to complete my act. I breathed once I finished and looked at their faces. The most senior looking guy walked up to me and patted on my shoulder quite strongly. He said I had made it to the second round. He then explained to me what I was supposed to do in the second round. The moment I stepped out of the audition room, I found Nitish and Satish sitting with unhappy faces. Now who would not know that it was because they had been rejected and I was selected, but I was sure they were more upset with their not so praiseworthy performances.

"Guys I have made it to the second round," I said. They remained expressionless and did not respond. "What guys? You are not happy for me?" I said and understood that they were lamenting for their failure and my success. "You guys are just…" I said an incomplete sentence and began walking away. After I walked a few steps, I felt a jerk and I found myself in air. Those two mad friends of mine had lifted me up in the air. Hundreds of college students caught that sight and

I felt so embarrassed. When they put me down, I gave them a nasty look but nothing could stop them and they went on.

"Dude, promise me you will not forget us after you become a star." Nitish said.

"Dude, the day you shift to Mumbai, you will allow us to visit you every week". Satish followed.

"Dude, promise me you will make me meet some huu-haaa hot actresses." Nitish said and became abnormal.

"Man I just want to go to these sense-killing parties to see what these pretty ladies look like in person," Satish blurted .

"Guys just shut up!" I burst out and they became silent.

"Can we focus on the next round now?" I kind of begged. I cleared the second round as well with ease. So far, I was the only one to have made it to the third round out of 200 students who were auditioned. The final round got over and I was the only one who cleared it. I was told that they were thinking of taking me for the lead role and I just needed to get some muscles in two months of time. The whole college took me as a star and I was enjoying it. For a second I thought if I became popular, Shreya might come back to me. But I shunned that thought as that would not be love for sure.

As far as my acting career was concerned, my photo never appeared in any magazine, I never attended a page 3 party, I never owned a bungalow at some posh location of Mumbai, no one talked about my link-up with any female actress, and I never signed an autograph for any fan. Ok, fine, let me not beat the bush any more. I couldn't become an actor. One day

I received a call and I was told that the producer of the movie was caught in casting couch, I shivered in my couch with this news and all my dreams shattered. Then I had such a bad time answering so many people, telling them I was no more going to be an actor. In the end Nitish and Satish consoled me saying they would produce a movie one day and give me the lead role.

ANOTHER DREADFUL DAY OF MY LIFE

I was lying on my bed one evening when my younger brother came running through the door and he was shivering badly. He looked totally scared, it gave me enough hint that something really bad had happened. It was indeed intimidating as my father was feeling a bad pain in chest. Immediately I called the doctor who was the custodian of my father's health and in a very worried tone I narrated the whole situation to him. His words shook the ground beneath my feet; he feared it was the symptom of a heart attack. The next moment we rushed him to the hospital, I had driven quite fast. In the hospital he was taken for ECG and several related tests and I felt the need of spending some time alone. I moved out of the hospital and sat on the stairs because it was not easy for me to walk normally. My mind flashed so many thoughts in that moment. Until this time I had always felt that I had lost all but now I realized I still had someone whose absence would finish me once and for all. I had never shared a cordial relation with my father, we always lived distinct lives. Never before had I tried to be close to him, to know him, to understand him. He was the one who played both the roles of a mother and a father for me after the demise of my mother. For several months he cooked for us, knowing we didn't enjoy the food made by the maid. He had done more than what any other father could just think of doing. I regretted for keeping him deprived of all the love that he deserved. At that moment, Love for him evolved fast in my heart as I watched traffic passing by on the road. Suddenly there was an unusual energy in me and I stood on my legs. I walked to a nearby temple where I prayed from my heart. I believed in God and by now everything was clear to me. Nothing was going to happen to my father in any case, God would never be so cruel. The whole incident was designed to sow seeds of love in the heart of a son. Maybe this is what my mother wished to see from that unknown place where she lived. After so many months I had felt the need of praying and that was very much a good sign. When you don't have anything to pray for, anything to ask for, life is not life. I was there praying profoundly for my father. Years of distances between us had destroyed the love between a father and son, but then that distance was getting curtailed in that moment. With no vagueness at all, I realized I had not been a good son till that day. I returned to the hospital. In my heart there was no trace of fear, not even a bit worry. I knew I was not going to lose my father; nothing could actually happen to him. My eyes were luminous and the news came exactly the way I had expected. It was no heart attack but just some gas that had moved up into his chest. Ever since that day I tried hard to give him less reasons to raise his eyebrows in matters relating to me. .Though I strongly advocate the thought that a father-son relation is somewhat naturally cursed, of course no hand in hand love, but hands in pocket and flare in eyes for each other.

THE MAD ASS

A few weeks later, when I returned home from college one day, I found Saurabh taking a peaceful nap on my bed and he had put on my clothes. I was startled to see him as he had not told me that he was coming to Delhi. But above all, the worst part about it all was that he had put on my clothes, like he did everytime he came to Delhi and I disliked it like always, but he never changed. I delivered a football kick on his ass that looked so big in my size Bermuda. I always felt his ass was not like a normal male ass; he had the ass of a big fat woman.

"Earthquake, earthquake!" he said as he jumped out of the bed.

I gave him a second to see me and when he did, I spoke, "Earthquake! Where? On your butt?"

"Oh man! It was you, you are such a…" he calmed himself.

"Shut up, you freak! What on earth are you here for at this time?" I asked. He overlooked me as he picked up his mobile phone and signaled me to be quiet. Immersed in bafflement, I watched him with my eyes becoming small in size.

"Ya muma, I am in hospital, yeah yeah I reached comfortably. Rohan? Ma just don't ask. He looks deplorable, too pale, and too weak. If you were here ma, you would have cried on seeing his face." Saying this he gave me a glance.

"What the fuck?" I whispered. There was a mirror right in front of where I stood. I looked into the mirror to scrutinize my face, though I was sure I was normal.

"Jaundice has taken a toll on his health, I pray he recovers fast!" He said further. I turned to him with a willingness to punch across his face this time. Jaundice and all his crap made me dizzy, I felt sick as if I was really a patient of jaundice.

"Now can I get a pinch of your attention or should I kick you on your ass again?" I said once he finished talking on phone.

"Hey man come sit, let me explain. I didn't tell you yet. I thought you were brainy enough to figure out yourself."

His expression changed and now he looked to be in some kind of day dream. After he made a long exaggerated sigh, he spoke quite cinematically.

"Dude I want this girl, she is making me insane, I am living my days and nights dreaming of her. It's not mere infatuation I tell you. I mean I never thought I would like her but ever since we started hobnobbing. I have liked her every single day." He stopped with his eyes fixed on the ceilings.

"Alright who is the girl this time?" I asked.

"It's Shruti. Shruti Chaudhary." His voice sounded lost.

"What that figure full of flab from our school, fatty chaudhary?" I reacted without measuring my words, with a slight touch of laughter. He took no offense at that comment by me. When I remembered my words, I made a quick effort to mean better.

"I mean she is like, really good. Very, very good. But how did it all happen? She is here in Delhi. You in Varanasi. I asked surprisingly."

"Oh! Facebook brought us this close. Besides we have been active on phone." His excitement rocketed.

"I strongly feel Shruti will just die without me." He said and I had a strong urge to laugh.

"Hey it's her sister's wedding tomorrow. She said it was ok if I came. So I am planning to give her a letter. I mean a love letter tomorrow night when we go there. What say?"

"Don't count me in. I am not coming with you." I expressed my refusal.

"Dude look don't do this. How am I going to do all this alone? We are best pals. Please come with me." He spoke in a begging tone.

"Look I have some work besides I don't like to go anywhere like this." I said as I tried to keep the real reason clandestine which was the possibility of seeing Shreya in the wedding. Shruti and Shreya were good friends.

"I know what makes you reluctant to come with me? It's Shreya. Believe me she is not here, She is not attending the wedding." I gave him a serious look this time. I have always detested his habit of being too blatant on all matters. As I looked at him, he made the face of a man who begs a brutal criminal for his life. I realized he was going to do all those irritating acts until I said yes. I surrendered with a nod. He jumped nearly four feet to hug me.

"You are such an asshole," I said.

AGAIN DRAGGED TO HER

Saurabh was ready with his love letter and a card that showed two babies kissing each other, it took him nearly 4 hours to draft a letter and decorate that card. He had named the two babies on the card as Saurabh and Shruti. Quite honestly he used a few drops of his blood too while writing that letter. However, the real reason was that he was suffering from bad gums and he made great use of his bleeding gums in writing a few lines of that letter. For the wedding couple, we had bought a triangular bouquet just to make ourselves appear like important guests. We reached the venue on time. Saurabh had grown freakier than ever, all in excitement, all for his fat love. He had turned into a girl who drivels steadfastly. It was a farm house wedding and all the arrangements were very lavish. Most of the guests were in formal ensemble other than us who were dressed for a picnic. We stood in one corner, gulping from our long glasses of coke, trying to feel comfortable.

"Dude. Who can have better luck than me? She seems to be rich; I mean I have never seen a wedding like this before. My father-in-law is a big man with 2 daughters only.

I will be the owner of half of his money. What a fortune?"
Saurabh murmured these lines on which I gave him a look
full of contempt. He called on Shruti's cell phone, talked like
a Hollywood hero, too confident. Shruti appeared before us
in no time; with kilos of foundation and talcum that doubled
and tripled her chubby face. After we congratulated her, I
handed her the bouquet; Saurabh passed her the card that had
the letter. Before he could say anything, her cell phone rang.
It was her mom's call, she went off after she excused herself.
Saurabh tried to stop her but she had been a little too fast
with her steps, so he failed. We realized she went off knowing
nothing about the card which had the letter and this could
lead to disaster. We followed her cautiously with our eyes; she
stopped near a lady who was supposed to be her mother. Our
hearts began jumping in our chests when we saw her going
away after giving the bouquet and the card to her mother.

"Fuck!" We whispered. Our gaze was still fixed on her
mother from our position. We saw her chatter with a few
guests, her hands still carried the bouquet, that card and that
letter which could get us killed. Abruptly, she placed the
bouquet on one round table. We expected her to leave the
card too along with the bouquet but the excessive decoration
of the card induced her to open it up.

"Damn!" we said in unison. Saurabh caught my right arm
out of fear with both his two arms and that scared me too.
She went through the card and then the letter, her expression
worsened while she read the letter. Those lines that he had
written using the blood from his gums were making full impact

on her mother. We both changed our direction, pretending to be in comfort.

"Dude its better if we run away from this place. It would be so humiliating to get thrashed in front of so many people." Saurabh spoke in nervousness and fear.

"Shut up and relax. If she has not seen us before, that means she can't catch us." I controlled the situation. For coming ten minutes we enjoyed our tomato soup and gave courage to each other, though unable to feel its taste because of the fiasco of everything.

Suddenly we heard a loud "Hello" from behind us. When we turned back, we saw Shruti's mother standing wide and tall with a broad smile on her face that appeared cruel on that occasion. It stunned both of us and we stood there without uttering any word in response.

"Hellooo," she repeated, in hope of a response this time. "Hello!" We said halfheartedly.

"You guys are Shruti's friends. I am Shruti's mother," she enquired cheerfully. We had been quite sure; she was trying to catch hold of the guy who used his blood to write a letter to her daughter.

"Oh! Hello aunty." We said with fake energy this time.

"What are your names?" She carried on with her casual enquiry.

I looked at Saurabh; I knew he acted dumb in bad situations. It was my past experience. Before he opened his mouth, I spoke hurriedly.

"Well I am Rohan and he is… Shatrughan." I wished I had taken a better name, quite instantly. Saurabh looked confused on knowing his new name. Even Shruti's mother looked unconvinced at his name as she waited for Saurabh's affirmation.

"I am Shatrughan, Shatrughan Sinha." He spoke with a lot of seriousness, I fought with a smile. She made a weird face and we were safe.

"You must be as tough as Shatrughan Sinha and that's why your parents gave you this name, I suppose," she said and smiled.

"No you got it wrong, they had actually seen one of his movies that night and then they…....."

"Ah! Anyway, congratulations aunty!" I kind of screamed to stop him from saying a word more. She looked at us with disgust for a few seconds and then she fought hard to bring that smile back on her face.

"Enjoy the evening." She said hesitatingly. We waited her to walk some distance away from us, and then we burst into laughter.

"Shatrughan Sinha," we said and laughed more. Soon after this, Shruti came to see us. And it was important that we told everything to her now. I was glad that Saurabh showed enough audacity to speak up; they began walking towards the exit. I followed them. They stopped under a tree covered with small light bulbs and where there was no one to see them except me. I became their audience standing ten meters away from them. Saurabh glanced in my direction, with all nervousness; I encouraged him by raising a thumb. They took nearly five minutes to become a couple; they finished with embracing each other. I began to walk away in order to give them their private moment. I reached the main entrance after a casual walk and then I saw something that could be anything but reality for me. I saw Shreya enter in a fully white costume. My mind was stunned, I felt something bizarre happening in my heart. I moved behind a tree before she could see me, I avoided a chance of encounter with her. She was over in my life, I had understood well. If I faced her again it was going to refresh all the pain. I looked at her till she walked far away; I judged I was losing self control. No matter how but I had erased her name from my heart, I had even flushed all the memories. In all confusion, I took out my cell phone and called Saurabh.

"You lied to me about Shreya," I spoke belligerently.

"Dude look I am sorry. I mean, is she here?"

"I am leaving now. Are you coming with me?" I avoided saying a word related to Shreya.

"Bro, just some more time, Shruti wants me to meet some of her friends. It won't take long. Just stay over for some more time. Please man...."

With some reluctance I replied, "Fine, I am out of this place now but I will be around, be quick." I exited and chose to take a slow walk on the road as there was hardly any vehicle at that time. It was a windy night and the light of the moon killed most of the darkness. I surely felt miserable. All those buried feelings were getting revived now. Life was playing games with me, undoubtedly. Someone's voice reached my ears and I did not take more than a second to feel that it was the voice of Shreya who called my name. I turned back. Shreya was coming towards me and soon her white face became clear into my eyes. Our eyes caught each other in silence.

"You should not be here," I said quite harshly. Her eyes retreated; she looked down at the ground. But I accentuated with bitterness in my eyes.

"I have something to say," she said in her soft voice which I heard after long.

"Just go," I snapped and avoided looking at her anymore.

"Please," she requested. Her voice had turned shaky.

"Go ahead. Say what you have to say," I casually allowed her to speak. Silence followed for a few seconds and then she spoke.

"I deserve your hatred for what I did with you. There is something that you don't know and suddenly I have no courage to tell you that. I pray every day that you get all the happiness of the world." Her voice became unstable. I could see beads of tears rolling down her cheeks. There was a sudden wind that hit us in that moment. For a second my hatred for her took a dive.

"I am finally doing what I always wanted to do, fashion designing and I have moved to Delhi now. Yeah, you were right it was not so impossible to convince a father." She spoke again after a pause. I prevented myself from getting carried away. I was sure of one thing this time; I was not going to allow myself to fall into any trap. My life was now important as I had people dependent on me. I gave her a heartless look.

"I believe you are done. I don't have a second more for you. Have a good life ahead," I said and walked away, leaving her behind. Saurabh stopped the car and I got inside after looking at Shreya, she stood at the same place.

Weeks passed on. I spent my days in thinking and nights in thinking more. I recalled every word that she spoke. She had indicated that she was not the same person who played with my feelings. She had given me enough wounds already and despite all that, I still grew curious to get the answers to a few questions. I phoned Saurabh, told him what I needed him to do. I wanted to know everything from Fatty, who was Shreya's friend and Saurabh's girlfriend. Saurabh gathered all relevant and irrelevant information in a few days during which I lived uneasily. Things that Saurabh told me left me open mouthed. Not even in my imagination I had expected to hear those things, I never thought that there could be a possibility of something like this too. For all these months, I thought Shreya was treacherous, she never loved me .Saurabh told me her love for me was never fake, in fact she had found her true love in me. The long hidden reality was that our love could not remain under tight wraps as Shreya's mother got a whiff of it. This was the time when Shreya got a real big shock. She got a wind of her father's liking for Prashant who was his closest friend's son,a third year student of MBBS. She was told that her father had always weaved plans for shreya and prashant, so this act of shreya was only going to devastate him. Those days had been nightmarish for Shreya. She had not really possessed the power to confront her father ever, nor did she want to hurt him. It was then that she chose to part ways with me, she chose to break the heart of the guy whom she loved madly. After living in pain for days, she made a decision to fight for what she wanted in life. It showed when she persuaded her father for fashion designing. I was confused, what to believe and what not. I thought it was all nonsense. Then I thought what if it was true, my heart trembled with all these thoughts. I asked myself a question, whether I still loved her. The answer was yes. I wondered what was going to happen. Now I was aware of the truth.

The very next day, out of my thundering desperation, I told my sister the whole story. I needed to see her reaction. It happens in life, over and over, no matter how independently we think and decide about our lives, we always need someone to take us out of certain situations. Besides my sister had always been my love advisor. So, even those late night programs on radio appear to be meaningful at times which are otherwise considered nothing but crap. Anyways, I told her everything that happened and she seemed pissed without saying any word at all. Here I am keen on enhancing your knowledge about female behavior. Unlike the opposite gender, they tend to first express their anger through silence, through their eyes, through their raised eyebrows. They do it to garner every bit of their energy for the wrestle next minute.

"Don't allow her to fool you again," she sort of screamed and I was startled as she rarely did such a thing. I told you we were like friends. I retreated like a frightened rat. She continued with belligerence.

"It's all bullshit and I really don't feel there is any truth in her story." With every word that she spoke, her voice rose.

"She is one of those girls who play games with morons like you. For God's sake, don't goof up again. Don't play with your life and ours like this." She ended up gazing deeper into my eyes. After a few minutes of silence I spoke to myself "She is right. I can't forgive her, I should not." She had once left me high and dry and there was no guarantee that she would not do it again.

LUT GAYE TERI MOHABBAT ME

It was festival season in all Delhi university colleges. Satish and Nitish had the right kind of information to make the best of it. They dug out that the most exciting fest happened in SRCC college and it had solely to do with exciting girls. Girls who wore fewer clothes, girls who showed most of their legs, only they could fit into the definition of exciting girls for my friends.

> *Tadap tadap ke iss dil se aah nikalti rahi*
> *Mujhko saza di pyaar ki aisa kya gunaah kiya*
> *Toh lut gaye, han lut gaye hum teri mohabbat me...*

KK was singing his most popular song and the crowd went bonkers. Nitish and Satish sang at the peak of their voices and so did the crowd. It was a song for all the heartbroken. I wondered if the whole place was full of ailing hearts. Nitish, in an attempt to make a video of KK's performances in his phone collided with a girl who called him rascal. He was upset, Satish and I laughed at him. Satish and Nitish danced pathetically. Their weird moves and steps caught the attention of many that included girls. They continued dancing happily in their own mad style knowing they were getting noticed by girls. I tell you they behaved as if they were drunk, but they were not, they were just mad. I had enjoyed something after a long time. After a round of freak style dancing, they did some more girl chasing. They wondered if I had some problem with my hormones as I never ran after girls. I had laughed. We were now leaving and then there was a pat on my back. I turned back and I saw Shruti. Shruti had come to catch KK live like us along with her friends. On seeing four good looking girls, I noticed their eyeballs jumped out and their mouth opened like that of a snake. They were craving for girls and more girls. They looked at each other and then at me. It was one of those looks saying "Great dude" I could tell looking at their faces what was going on in their minds. I introduced Nitish and Satish, they actually demanded through their eyes, Shruti too introduced her friends. The guys initiated an unnecessary handshaking ceremony and they held the hands of the girls for extra seconds. Shruti fought with a smile, she looked at me, and I looked around. After all it was my friends who behaved as if so far they had lived on a planet with no girls and only now they were seeing them. In all this, Shruti spoke, "Rohan I want to have a word with you in private." Nitish and Satish looked at me with the same action, quite robotically. I thought they performed some kind of group dance.

"Go Rohan, go, go! Come on, go." They said repeatedly. I knew what was on their minds. Shruti laughed and her friends too. We walked a few meters away.

"It's about Shreya." She spoke quite too seriously.

"Yeah. What?" I was full of nonchalance. She raised her pitch to get me serious. No doubt she succeeded.

"Look I know she has given you a lot of pain but I believe you know all the reasons behind what she did. Look I know that somewhere you still love her. Please, she is very unhappy. Just think again." I heard scrupulously, and I spoke no word in reply. We walked back, Satish and Nitish tried hard to create an impression on Shruti's friends.

"Guys let's leave," I kind of ordered. Shreya was on my mind now. Faces of my friends turned sad. They wanted to be with the girls for the rest of their lives. They kept turning back to wave at them. Nitish repeatedly screamed "bye pinky". There was no girl with the name Pinky, I thought. We hired an auto, and the guys were finding it hard to control their excitement. I made the mistake of sitting in the centre, they were going mad. "Dude just because of you I met Pinky," Nitish said

"Who is Pinky?" I asked.

"Oh Pinky is Priyanka, she is my Pinky. I asked her if I could call her Pinky. She agreed. Now Niti and Pinky, they are soul mates. Nitipinki, Pinkiniti, Pinkiniti, Nitipinki. He made a song." When Nitish finished, Satish began.

"Preeti, what a girl! Soft, sweet, *sushil*."

I wondered if he was going to call her Sushila like Pinki. Satish and Sushila.

READY TO SHED TEARS AND DRINK BEER

It was the next day, rather next night. Shruti's words had worked to disturb my mental stability in the whole matter. Soon I realized it, what Shreya did was perhaps the best thing one can do. She never played with my heart. In that precise moment, while thinking all this I decided one thing. I decided to bring her back into my life. Whether I was right or wrong, I left it on God. I was ready to shed tears and drink beer in case she hurt me again. With all seriousness now I had understood the importance of family. I was not going to give them even the slightest of pain ever again. No matter what happened in my own personal life. So finally I was ready to pursue my love which had been unfortunate till now. I wanted to call her and talk right away, and so I obtained her cellphone contact. Excitement roared, heart wobbled, I felt lost. I called her with alot of hesitation. Suddenly there was that old hello. She said hello again as I could not break my silence. I realized I was required to speak but before that could happen; the line got disconnected due to my balance reaching nil. My balance had got over at the wrong time. I was bemoaning from inside, even she didn't call back. After a few seconds it dawned on me that I had free messages in my phone. Our exchange of words on text was something like this.

Me: Hiii!

Shreya: Do I know you?

Me: No doubt you do. You know me well.

Shreya: Even if you are someone I know, it would be very kind of you if you allow me to do my work… bye…

Me: What if I say I am not going to be kind with you…

Shreya: Are you mad?

Me: Yeah, only someone mad can do that.

(I was enjoying our chat thoroughly)

Shreya: What nonsense?

Me: Yeah exactly. There is no sense in leaving home, catching train, drinking beer… all for a girl…

Shreya: Rohan???

Me: Naah… That mad guy

Shreya: I am sorry, I was not expecting you.

Me: Expecting someone else?

Shreya: No!!

Me: I know…

Shreya: What?

Me: Nothing. Are you free to meet on any day?

Shreya: This is all a surprise.

Me: How about tomorrow? (I didn't allow her to fix our meeting in the distant future. I didn't want any tossing on bed during nights. It happens when you want something from the bottom of your heart, you lose your sleep.

I waited for her at City Square Barista. The place was full of couples, a lot more than usual. I was a little before time like always whenever it was about meeting her. There was some event going on by way of making mall visitors sing a song of their choice. When she reached, she was before time too. I helped her with her chair though it was well understood that she was not really my girlfriend at that time. We both sat on our seats in very slow motion as if we both were in favor of a hug instead of sitting doron. No movement was made as my eyes triggered its searching task on her face, in her eyes, on her calm lips. Eye talk session got over and I spoke.

"So now we have a story worth remembering for life, I am nourishing plans of writing a book on us. All thanks to you for giving me plenty of things to write about." It was an attempt to make her laugh but it only dimmed the light on her face. I hated myself for messing up with my attempt to strike a conversation. Considering that it was nothing more than a reunion ceremony for two people in love and so it was supposed to go the simplest way. I straightened on my chair, placed my hand on her hand, she looked into my eyes.

"Look now I know everything and I must say it's very rare to find a girl like you." I said.

"But I caused you so much of pain," she said as she looked down. It generated a stronger urge in me to take her into my arms.

"But you loved me always and only that matters," I said with an attempt to influence her. She remained mouth zipped.

"I still love you like those days." This was my spontaneous use of words that came out uncontrollably.

"I have missed you every single day since we parted." She spoke after taking a few minutes.

"Great, so dare not make this mistake again. See, you are a shopaholic mammal and only I can be your trolley with maximum capacity." I said to bring that smile back on her face. My heart felt relieved.

"Do you intend to complain because you carried all my shopping bags once?" She asked and laughed.

"No, I only intend to take immense pleasure," she smiled with her eyes dimmed by tears.

"I love you, Rohan," she said in a weepy tone. I took her right hand between both my hands and placed a soft kiss to comfort her.

Suddenly our attention was drawn by someone singing absolutely out of tune. It was a love song which the guy performed with deep feelings, no doubt it was dedicated to the girl he loved.

"Something special today," I said quite absently.

"Valentine's Day." She replied instantly. I turned my head to face her in complete shock. Her smile was still there.

"Valentine's day…" I sort of faltered.

"You are a mad human being." I murmured to myself. She was aware of what was going on inside me.

"I have you and I have all." She tried to make me feel it was no mistake that I had no clue about Valentine's Day. My sadness subsided and with that came the great idea. I jumped on to my feet with an unusual energy and style, grabbed her hand and walked to the center of the mall where guys and girls were singing for each other. In a minute I had the mike in my hand, Shreya stood a few meters away and hundreds of people had their eyes fixed on us. It was because of years of participation in school assembly and debate competitions that kept all nervousness at bay.

"Well it's Valentine's Day… I am sure all you boyfriends must have showered roses and gifts on your girlfriends. I am just so devastated; I have no gift for that girl standing there, not even an indispensable rose." The crowd made a haaaww sound; even those who were on other floors gave their attention to me. In no time I connected with most of the mall visitors, I am sure they were seeing this kind of madness in reality for the first time.

"So I have a song for her and just a song. Only if she likes, I will be relieved." I carried on confidently. The crowd was enjoying and making more noise, Shreya stood there in all shyness. The guy responsible for making announcements informed our names to the crowd after he asked me.

"This one's only for you Shreya, from this mad fellow in love." The crowd put their volume down, all for my song. I took a deep breath and began.

"Oceans apart day after day and I slowly go insane I hear your voice on the line, but it doesn't stop the pain If

I see you next to never, how can we say forever. Wherever you go, whatever you do I will be right here waiting for you Whatever it takes or how my heart breaks, I will be right here waiting for you…"

My song echoed and stunned the crowd. As far as my girl was concerned, now she wasn't shy, she looked at me with a smile on her face that said many things.

"I took for granted all the times that I thought wouldlast somehow, I hearthelaughter, I tastethetears, butI can'tgetnearyou now Oh can't you see it, Baby, you've got me going crazy.

Wherever you go, whatever you do I will be right here waiting for you Whatever it takes or how my heart breaks I will be right here waiting for you…"

My eyes closed with the last line and the crowd began with a noisy applause. Then I bent my right knee; spread my arms in the direction of Shreya. She took a few steps towards me by covering her mouth with both her hands in bafflement.

"Be mine forever." I pleaded, looking at her.

"Forever…forever." She responded immediately.

I stood up, grabbed her hand and walked out of the mall. As we walked out, the crowd made a lot of noise, whistles, hooossss and hoye hoyeess. I bought a rose for her which she accepted with a gorgeous smile.

"You actually have singing talent. You should at least give it a try."

"Oh! Forget."

"Why forget it?" From walking along she just came in front of me to block my way; it startled me. Here I would take the honor to reveal a very important fact. It's a basic fact that girls are the most stubborn creatures in the whole universe.

"I am not so flawless in singing but I always wanted to try." I said with a bit of grief in my words.

"Exactly, you should keep on trying."

"But dad," I said irritatingly.

"What is it with dad now?"

"It's just that I was doing early morning practice one day. My father was quite not enjoying it. He came up to me to make it clear that I was wasting my time in something crass and I should better indulge in something good. He called me a train singer."

"Who is a train singer?" She asked with a grimace.

"Oh! Forgive me for not explaining the term 'train singer'. These are the singers seen in tattered clothes, unlike their counter parts in Bollywood. They have to have a disorder. Blind or deaf, mostly. If you travel in sleeper class coaches, chances are high you would meet these train singers." She burst into laughter, I laughed too.

"No doubt you are a good singer but I think you are great in storytelling. You can be a great writer." she chuckled.

"O! yes and I already have a story to share." I winked at her. She bit her lips to kill me with the sharpness of her features. We walked hand in hand along the busy roads for the rest of the time; life was again full of delight.

NOT JUST CA BUT MBA TOO

Only a few days had passed, Shreya asked me about how I was doing in Chartered Accountancy. Here I would like to give you a dose of reminder; I had chosen CA as career for Shreya as she was doing MBBS then. She left me and I left CA despite cracking the foundation exam with no effort at all. My father understood that his son was not made to do a course like CA and so he did not force me to be serious about it.

But anyways, she had made a re-entry in my life. Now she pursued fashion designing, but I needed to know the answer to a big question. Was I supposed to push myself further into CA ? I tried to know from Shreya if being a CA would make it any easy at the time of confrontations with her parents? She answered in affirmative. She explained that I needed to do better than Prashant (her father's closest friend's son) and Prashant was a medical student too. I paid attention to her words, and then I blew a good quantity of hot air from my mouth.

I mean was it easy to surpass the achievement of a doctor? Who can ever be better than people who save lives? Only god could be. For a second I thought Shreya woke up to this fact, only in a dream I could do better than a doctor.

"How about MBA?" She spoke enthusiastically.

I thought she realized it. Two years of MBA was more feasible for someone like me who had already wasted a few years where CA was concerned. That moment I thought she was a brave girl who decided to tough out things when they happened in future. Perhaps she was going to persuade her father for an MBA degree holder, no doubt after she summoned a lot of courage. But there is a barrier to communication, it's premature listening. If you don't allow the speaker to complete, it will happen with you.

"Look you just need to drag your maths to perfection and I am sure you will crack a very good MBA college." She knew how I had messed up in maths in the last few years due to lack of practice.

"Oh ya I need to, I will start working on maths right away." I assured her with interest.

"So CA + MBA is just so cool," she spoke, her voice was dreaming.

What? CA + MBA? Did she just say CA + MBA? I was doubtful about my hearing powers, "CA +MBA." I spoke chicken heartedly.

"Yeah isn't that a great combo? I have heard that it is." Her words thrilled me. I breathed uneasily, my head began to dance. From a horse I felt like an ass, an ass whose life was going to get screwed. I made a quick calculation in my mind and the outcome made me dizzy. I was going to become an old man chasing this CA + MBA target. After a few seconds spent in silence, I opened my mouth, "Oh ya it is. It is… CA + MBA. It is… it's great… it's good…" My heart cried. But this CA+MBA gave her a reason to be positive for, so I was not going to disappoint her. Had I shared my plans with my father, he would have looked for a mental hospital for me that provided shock therapy. I was his son who was behaving like nuts. Now, it was time to march ahead in CA and in love with Shreya. We would meet every day, roam, go to pubs, go to markets where she would shop, but I would feel more than her trolley now. You would wonder how I survived a heavy rain of expenditure over my head, but *Dost, dene wala jab bhi deta, deta chappar faad ke*. I had found a weekend job in Gurgaon. It was about conducting surveys in UK over the telephone, pay was handsome for 8 days of work in a month, besides they offered fabulous incentives on doing greater number of surveys. I would beseech and beg the old men and women in UK for their help in my surveys. I know they were English and they ruled on us. But I found them quite friendly and cordial. I wondered why their grandfathers and fore fathers were so full of brutality; anyways I worked hard on weekends, labored for CA exam in weekdays, and had fun with Shreya to the maximum. She appreciated all the hard work I was doing for her and that would provide worth to my hard work.

2'o CLOCK TRING TRING

How many of you believe that happiness comes and goes? And of course, then it comes again. Clearly speaking it never stays on for too long. I don't know why it is like this but then it's the rule of God I sometimes feel.

That night I had already consumed four mugs of coffee as I struggled with one big accountancy problem that continued to torture me badly so I planned to sleep. Before catching sleep I sent a text message to Shreya saying I love you. Shreya would never be up till so late but she was in habit of reading my message the moment she opened her eyes in the morning. She would demand for this, girls make many such absurd demands all the time. But at the same time I would find happiness in doing that because these things showed she really loved me. Keeping other things aside, I would go on to tell you what terrible thing happened that night. I sent her a text message and tried to sleep. Exhaustion and long hours of slogging off on table, both worked as I slid into sleep very quickly. Breaking all silence, my cell phone that lay next to my pillow rang and at that moment it shook me in sleep like an alarm. It was totally an unexpected call that broke my sleep. I reached over for my phone with high irritation and it was a call from an unknown number. I picked up.

"Who?" I asked in a sleepy tone.

"You will know but first tell me your address." It was a heavy and husky voice of a middle aged man. My sleep faded a bit as it was strange that someone was asking me for my address at 2'o clock night.

"I think you are buzzing on the wrong line." My voice had a touch of exasperation.

"Address." Reply came in a word after a few seconds in a clear and louder voice. It shocked me quite terribly, my anger jacked up.

"Fuck off." I said.

"Address?" The man said again. This was heights and I was already bugged to the maximum. I told him the address and as soon as I did, the call was disconnected from his end. Clearly it was nonsensical to expect a man on the door at such an odd timing and I dozed off.

Early morning my phone rang again. It was Shreya. I picked and said "Good Morning!" with my voice full of sleep. For a minute when she did not reply I realized there was surely something wrong and I slowly scrambled out of my sleep.

"Shreya you there? Is everything ok?" I asked with fear growing in me.

"Dad read your last night's message." I realized her father was in Delhi to attend a seminar.

"What? How?" I was so frightened that I stood up on the bed. I gulped.

"I was giving him a head massage in his room quite late at night and I left my phone on his bed. I returned to my room and slept as it was late. He woke me up, he looked very angry. He said just one line "Now I know why you are here in Delhi?" I don't know, what is going to happen. His anger is bad. I am damn scared Rohan." I heard her without an expression. And I thought about that call last night. I checked the details and I had got this call at 2. Things were getting clearer, about that call, and about all. I asked Shreya to tell me her father's cell phone number. She did and it matched with the number on my screen.

"Oh damn!!!" My voice quivered. "He was the one who called me last night."

"What are you saying?" Shreya said furiously. He did call me after he read that message. I gave her full confirmation that we were soon going to face danger. The whole conversation from last night became fresh in my mind. Not exactly the whole but my twice use of the 'f' word. I was bemoaning inside. Even if it was unintentional, it was a big enough offense. In films, I had seen a hero going to any extent to prove himself to the heroine's father who would mostly play villain. Though, he would succeed in the end in winning the heart of the villain father. In my case, the hero had ruined all his chances. If he showed his face to the heroine's father ever again, he would only get killed. And the heroine would be forced to marry someone else. I just wanted to bang my head on the wall. It was worse than anything I could imagine.

"What happened Rohan?" Shreya asked over and over. I found myself in a tight spot, danger could knock at my door any minute. My heart sank, it almost stopped.

"Is your dad home? Just check, hurry," I asked my voice fumbled.

"Why? What happened?" Girls have this worst habit of asking questions even when you are dying.

"Shreya please don't ask questions. Just do as I say or I will be dead."

"Ok, ok, fine." I was thankful to her for not asking me any more questions at that time. There was silence on the phone as she went to check. Every part of my body, whether external or internal, was growing uneasy. How desperately I wanted Shreya to find her father at home. She tortured my heart by taking somewhat around ten minutes to find out where her father was. And when she was back, she had the answer which had the effect of acid.

"He isn't here." She said with no clue of what it actually meant.

"FUCK!" I was getting mad.

"What?" She hated whenever I used this 'f' word.

"No, no Fuck! I am sorry." I was losing my mind. "Did you check the bathrooms?"

"Yeah I did."

"Garden?"

"We don't have a garden Rohan. It's a society flat."

"Store room?"

"Why do you think he would go to the store room?"

"Oh yeah, why should I think he would go to the store room, but if he is nowhere then, that means he is coming here to give me his love and blessings."

"What are you saying?" She sounded like she was highly irritated. And never irritate a girl too much. So I chose to explain.

"Look Shreya, last night he called me at 2 and simply asked my address. The call made no sense to me ,but, I ended up giving him my address."

"Oh my God!!" She said realizing only God could help. "That means he is out and he is coming to your house."

"Very much, yes." We both, terrified. Next moment, I could hear her cry. It poured fear in my heart. Perhaps, she knew her father was now going to make a million pieces of her lover. For fathers their daughters are their world. So they could go to any extent, they could even take someone's life, and someone like me definitely deserved to be killed from the point of view of a daughter-driven father. Shreya was already sobbing. If I told her the worst thing that happened, that I used 'F' word talking to her father, her fear would turn into anger. She would kill me with one question? "How could you make such a mistake?" I would reply "why on earth would a guy get a call from the father of the girl he loves at 2'o clock night?" She would repeat her question, I would repeat my answer. Then again, suddenly her father would get his hand on me. And I would take my last breath. So I decided to tell her nothing.

"Shreya, look we have got to handle this. Please control yourself. I will give you a call in a short while; let me see what I can do now." While I was about to disconnect the call she whispered I love you. I suddenly felt strong. "Don't worry, nothing will happen. I love you too."

I took a deep breath. At first, I went to check on my father. He was almost ready to leave for work. My sister had already left for her classes. The only one left was my brother now, though I was sure that he would have left for his school but I still went to his room to check. I was befuddled to find him on his bed. Hurriedly I woke him up. I asked him why he was missing his school. He, not too confidently, said "Fever". I touched his forehead; it was cool. I took no time to understand, he was fooling me. He would barely hide a thing from me. So he accepted, he had not completed his homework and the teacher was strict. I had no time, so I just gave him an angry look and asked him to leave the bed. I went to the main door, locked it up. Then I waited for my father to leave. Usually, he left early; but that day he was being too slow. Once he left, we moved out of the house. My younger brother was puzzled. He was clueless about what was happening. We went to the park which was right in front of my house and hid behind a tree. There were cars passing by and I prayed that none of them stopped near my house. After ten minutes or so, a white

Santro stopped at the entrance of our lane. The man who drove it looked like a driver; the man who sat next to him was my father in law in dream. But unfortunately he was behind my ass, and in fact everything at that moment. The car had stopped; the driver rolled down his window and tried to figure out the house. Within five minutes they reached, the driver remained inside and the danger man got out of the car. He was a charming person; had got to be Shreya's father. When my brother saw him, he asked me who he was. I candidly told him that he had come to kill me.

"Have you fought with someone?" he asked.

I replied "No, I simply loved someone." He looked utterly bewildered. I had been incredulous, her father was really there. What exactly was his plan to do with me? Had he seriously come to take my life? Or just to threaten me. He stood on the gate for a while, and then went inside through the main door which had been unlocked. The door inside was locked. So he came out soon. His body language suggested that he was seething with rage. We had fixed our eyes on him, from our positions behind the tree. Then, he took out his cell phone and my phone buzzed. I took it out hazily and silenced it. I preferred not to reject. Rejection would have been another offence. He called again and it went unpicked. Then he left. I sat down where I had so far stood. I heaved a sigh of relief. Shreya had been calling me and I told her everything that happened. She heard me in numbness. Totally petrified. I told her everything was fine so for. But her father would be more pissed now after having failed to find her daughter's lover. It could fuel to the fire in him. He was surely going to make it worse for us, perhaps the worst.

My anticipation proved to be correct, Shreya called me again to shock me with the dizzying news that her father was taking her to Varanasi; they were catching an evening flight. That was four hours from then. I turned mournful. Surprisingly, she was the one who showed courage at that time. She made me feel a little better by saying "No one can separate us now." She said it was her turn to prove her love.

SHAHRUKH KHAN FACES AMRISH PURI

Dusk was falling. Soon, my love would go away from me. My eyes were habituated to see her face every day. I was turning into a freak and my heart lived with a very weird kind of pain, inexplicable pain. Such a crazy feeling I tell you, I could have really chosen to become a terrorist at that moment as I was totally off my nut.

Her flight was at 7 in the evening and for a second I thought of catching the same flight. Working part time had given me enough savings. I could easily afford an air ticket now. But that thought vanquished the moment Shreya's father came to my mind. He would definitely kill me in the flight itself in case he suspected me of being his daughter's lover.

He would then throw my dead body from a height and I am scared of heights. I can't even imagine it happening to my dead body. I can die for my love but such a death is not acceptable to me. All those warm-blooded heroes ought to take a lesson here, playing cool and safe is the key to love. I gave up on that idea, made myself understand that I had to live without her till she came back to me. I remembered her promise; she was going to come back to me soon. I trusted her.

I took a glance at my wrist watch, it was 6. I found myself at the airport. I believe I don't owe an explanation here; I would do anything to see her. Through a text message I enquired and got to know that my girl was reaching the airport in ten minutes along with the danger man. They reached shortly and Shreya had no clue that I would already be there to see her. I had waited near the refreshment shop while I saw them take a seat in the waiting lounge. In all worries, a smile found its place on my face; she was in front of my eyes. I had been at the airport and so was the girl of my dream, I felt the urge of flying to some far place with her where her father would never reach nor anyone else. But surely there were so many obstacles in doing that. My savings had been quite meager, this time my sister and father would not embrace any excuse for my running away. If the danger man found his daughter missing at the airport he would straight away go to my house and meet another danger man, my father. They would join hands against me. So the bottom line was, two danger men to fight in the end. So I gave a strict no to my idea of flying with the girl. I had been very close to her, sipping coffee and looking at her. Five minutes passed, her father stood up, I guess to empty his bladder. He walked towards the restrooms, I moved from my place. As I seated on the empty seat to her right, I made sure to make no sound. She had buried herself in a magazine that was shockingly the *Outlook*. A girl reading *Outlook* or *Frontline* was so unimaginable. Being a guy, I only read *Stardust* and other such magazines.

"Aren't you missing me?" I said. She closed her book unsteadily and turned right.

"Rohan you are…God you have no idea what can happen here?" She said in extreme fear.

"I know.. I know.. That man in the loo will kill me in case he catches me here but I am not afraid of dying". I said

"Look, cut out the crap and go." She ordered in high degree panic.

"Ok fine I am going. Handle everything and get back soon. Don't leave me again." I said and placed my hands on both sides of the chair to finally get up. Suddenly something happened to her and she placed her hand on mine. It was her time to get emotional, to shed some tears.

"Look please don't, you are not going to cry else I will book a ticket in the same flight and come with you." I said with fear in my heart. Seeing her cry would be something very painful, I felt in that moment. Still she shed a few tears, pearl like tears, on her cheeks. One can't stop a girl from crying when she wants to.

"Hey why are you giving me pearls. I am no jeweler." I said.

"What?" She smiled in tears.

"Oh yes they are no less than pearls. Don't waste them." I said in a soft voice. I wiped off her tears with my fingers and pleaded her for a smile.

"Now hurry up; leave, it's dangerous if you stay here a minute more." She said.

"Take care; I will be waiting for your call." I said as I stood up to leave.

"I will soon, now just leave for home." She said. Then it was the turn to exchange those words that serve the finishing words in love. She said I love you, with a lot of intensity.

"I love you like mad." I replied as I began to walk away from her, but my head was turned towards her. Suddenly I banged into someone, someone heavy. I was still busy saying I love you to Shreya. That collision took place because I did not see where I was going.

"Sorry." I uttered to that supposedly stranger. My head had still been bent low after the bang, when I raised my head I almost fainted at the sight. The word FUCK rolled into my mouth. Shahrukh khan was facing Amrish Puri, I was facing her father. For a second I thought of running away but it would have looked odd had I done that, especially with Shreya around me. I was her man, and a man never runs away from a situation. Now let's talk about her father. He was on the verge of becoming a werewolf with his teeth clenched. There were so many people around us but I felt I was alone and now no one could save me. I looked back at Shreya, and then looked at him again. Shreya was up on her feet; despite a few meters of distance between us I could still hear her heartbeats. The word hear should not be used, but surely I could feel her heartbeats. It raced like the wheels of Schumacher's car. I gulped, she gulped and the danger man was ready for the pulp. It was totally his wish to have the pulp or prefer a shake rather. Suddenly I heard his voice, bitter and sharp. It made me wonder if he had been having only neem leaves.

"So you dared to do this? You are following us!" He said. "No sir, I am not daring at all. I mean I am daring. I can really follow you and your daughter anywhere, even to the bathroom. But this happened by mistake. I made no plan at all of standing in front of you like this. I just wanted to steal a few glimpses of your daughter, your beautiful daughter. Go catch your flight and let me leave too." I wanted to say all that, in fact with folded hands but I stood there without a word. At this time when I looked at Shreya, she gave me a look as if I had already been beaten up by the danger man. I should have realized that any eye contact with his daughter could have infuriated him further. In a flash he moved from his position and I could not stop myself from giving a look at his daughter again, no matter what the danger man felt. Shreya looked like her mouth would open but before it happened I felt a blow on my right chest. I wore a t-shirt that read "touch me if you can" and that t-shirt was almost into his right hand. I was thankful to months of work out that gave me pretty tight muscles on the chest and he didn't really hurt me. But the way he held my t-shirt, I felt like a Mahabharata character who had once offended a Kaurava and later the same Kaurav was keen on taking revenge. I am talking about Draupadi. I indeed felt like Draupadi.

"Dad please. Listen." She spoke.

"You better save your words for now." He snapped at her. Now it was a scene, a bad one, most of the people around us now saw all this happening. Who would want to miss the scene of a lover facing savagery. I searched for words that I could possibly use to save myself. There was a line using which

I could have avoided all the drama. And that line was "Sir. Please don't take me wrong, your daughter is like my sister." But the fact was that we both loved each other. I would die but not do something like that to save myself.

"You know who I am?" He shouted for hundreds to hear. I felt he could have asked that question quite decently and I would have answered quite respectfully. My answer would have been somewhat like this.

"Sir you are the best doctor we have in Varanasi. It's because of you that people of Varanasi are alive. You are not an ordinary man sir, you are like God you are great." But the way he yelled his question, no one could say that he expected an answer from me.

"I have great links. You have no idea what I can do to you." He said in a high pitch. I stood there in silence, waiting for him to take his hand off my t-shirt. Suddenly I saw a few policemen; they asked if there was a problem. They asked her father, not me. They were actually there to simplify his job, do the rest of it. Now if you recall, I have already spoken about how badly I hate policemen. So now for the first time in life I was going to encounter them.

"This guy has been chasing us everywhere." He said it to those fat looking policemen. Now that was a pure lie. I chased his daughter a few times, not even once had I chased him. But even that statement would not have saved me. Rather saying it, I would testify my crime, crime from their perspective. "Dad please". Shreya tried to open her mouth again. But he gave her a nasty expression and it made her mum. Had I wanted,

I would have clarified to those policemen that I was in love with her and that even she loved me too. The whole situation would have been different. Of those three policemen, the one with the best round shaped belly walked towards me. He held my left arm with his right hand, quite strongly. "Please no." Shreya screamed, on the verge of breaking down. She even tried to move closer to me but the danger man stood like a wall between us.

"I believe you don't want me to make it worse for you. We are late for our flight. Come with me now." He said in his favorite bitter tone. The next moment our eyes met, I asked her to leave, do as her father wanted. With a smile I tried to make her believe that those policemen were not going to hurt me or take me to jail, rather they were taking me to some spa where I could relax. In reality I had envisaged the kind of spa treatment I was going to get, where my hands were tied up over my head, shirt removed, jeans too, then a bad tempered policeman who is chewing a pan comes close to me with a thick wooden stick made of forest wood. She was walking away with her father, doing what I had asked her. I was trying to apply force against those policemen who caught me strongly, making me feel like a terrorist. But love and terror, are similar in some ways. She kept on turning back, I saw her wet eyes, it pained in that moment. If I had not feared a bullet in my back, I would have kicked in between the legs of that policeman and run to give her a hug. But I would not do anything that could put my life in danger. I had a dream and I had to get it sensibly. The dream was to spend my life with Shreya, to see her face every morning, to take a towel from her hand every time I went bathing, to taste soup from her hands every time I fell sick, to tease her for fun just to love her more the next minute. With a turn, she went out of my sight. I had shown enough patience till now. In that moment I thought if I really had links with Taliban or Afghanis, I would have taken their help to hijack the plane that my love was going to board. I would drop her father on some unknown island, in fact everyone, and then I would fly away with her. I guess I have already talked about its repercussions, and why I dropped that plan. Anyways I had to deal with Delhi police now.

TEA, TOILET AND TERROR

Sitting inside the police van, I thought about my mother. When I was a kid she had taught me a galaxy of things like good deeds, bad deeds and that the latter could lead you to jail. I was wondering if I had really committed a crime for which I was about to land up in jail. The answer was no way an affirmative. I was not a criminal. But it really did not matter, whether I was a criminal or not, I was surely in trouble. I badly needed to think of something to take myself out of the situation. Calling my father did not come to my mind, I was sure of getting no help from him. Besides he would have worsened the situation for me by making a few declaration like, I would no longer be allowed in his house, I had lost all the rights over his property. He would even say I was no more his son . So I decided not to call him. My sister was next and surely she was not going to deny that I was her brother, but still I had so many apprehensions in calling her.

Her what? How? Why? And again, what? How? Why? would collect a thousand people around her. It gave me a thrill to think about the quantum of defamation that would come my way. No shopkeeper would give me a packet of bread and eggs without asking me about my jail experience, no mother would let her daughter stand in the balcony in fear of my passing by (of course I would not be concerned with any girl on any balcony but still it was bad), even street dogs would bark at me. But it was important that I informed her. A few minutes before reaching police station, one of the policemen asked me if I was a local guy or an outsider. Now, had I told them the truth, no doubt they would have summoned my father or sister and I would die out of shame in case that happened. My father or sister would come rushing to the police station where they would see me locked up. I thought of a good answer that could even be helpful in that situation. I lied that my parents lived in Varanasi and I was a student preparing for civil services examination. I further said that I wanted to become an IPS officer. For once they looked at each other and then at me. I desperately hoped that my trick worked on them. If they saw a future IPS officer in me, they would not torture me the way they would otherwise do. Soon I found myself at Mahipalpur police station. My heart began to beat faster; I wondered what was going to happen to me. I followed them inside with enormous fright, almost quivering. Now inside, there was a table with a register (must be complaint register), a man who sat on the floor in one corner and one policeman who seemingly crushed tobacco in his hands, he had put on a white vest as if he was in his bedroom. He asked the two policemen about me. They avoided his question casually, I then felt may be they had understood that it was not good for them if they messed up with a future IPS officer. I was asked by one of the policemen to sit on the floor, next to the man who was already sitting there. I cursed myself breathlessly for getting myself trapped into a situation like this. I sat down reluctantly. The other guy slowly glanced up, our eyes met. He asked me about my crime, I got to know he had beaten up his wife. Now how ironical it was; I was sitting there because of my madness in the pursuit of getting the wife of my choice, whereas he was sitting there because he had beaten up his wife, so irksome. I turned my face away from him. It had got very late. I realized on taking a look at my wrist watch. I asked a policeman if I could make a call, he allowed it. I called my sister facing the wall. I lied that I was at Nitish's place attending his birthday and it was likely that I would stay at his place over night. I heard someone's scream from a terrible beating, I turned fear stricken. I assumed my turn to be the next. When my sister asked about that sound, I told her it was the time to cut the cake. I disconnected the call and returned to the floor, with terror in my heart. The policeman continued to beat that man, brutally, targeting his ass. I thought I had never seen a swollen ass before. But then surely I was going to experience it myself. The other man was beaten almost to death; I was pretty sure that now he would touch his wife only for one reason, after getting this treatment he would never dare to beat her again. The man in vest noticed me now, I noticed him too with reluctance. He motioned to me to get up and he sat on a chair at some distance. I got up using my right hand, though my bones had been shaky. He looked at me carefully and asked the details of the whole matter. That was mystifying, a policeman was asking for explanation. But that

was really something in my favor. I told him blatantly, I was
no miscreant but a student aspiring to become an IPS officer.
About the girl, I said I loved her and that the girl loved me too.
About her father, I said I hated him as he came in between
us. While I was speaking, he asked me to sit down. I seated
with the thought that at least now I would not get thrashed
up. It was unexpected, getting such treatment without being
a minister or any other man of high position. He asked me if
I was seriously in love with the girl. I found his question very
interesting. I told him that I was mad about her ever since that
night in train. He looked confused, and then asked me about
the night in train. I told him it was a long story but he insisted
on knowing. Refusing a policeman could be really hazardous
for me, moreover he was being so lenient with me, so courteous.
I began telling him about that train journey, about that night.
To hear my story, three more policemen joined us, those were
the ones who had held me at the airport and brought me to
police station. When I paused after the story of the first train
journey, they showed eagerness to know more. One old man
put four white cups of tea for the four policemen, the man
in the vest asked him to fill in one more cup for me. I was
enjoying the hospitality. With the cup in my hand and a sip at
regular intervals, I told them how I managed to propose to her
in train. They all heard me quite cheerfully, like the way you
see a movie. My story had reached to its sad junction. How
she changed one day. Suddenly my phone rang; it was Shreya.
By air, it takes just one and a half hour to reach Varanasi from
Delhi. So she had reached. I picked without wasting a second,
in front of those policemen.

"Where are you? Those policemen? What did they do with you?" She bombarded me with so many questions. And I knew she was crying.

"Hey, hey, hey, Shreya. Please stop crying. I am okay; just fine," I spoke hastily.

"You are lying," she said

"Oh no. I am not. Do I sound like I am badly beaten up?" I said looking at those policemen.

"So are you home then? You got rid of those policemen easily?" She asked again.

"No, no I am still in the police station." I replied.

"What? If you are still in police station, how come you are fine? Have they put you in a cell? Her questions kept flowing."

"I am not in any cell. I am sitting with those policemen. We are just…" I said with a struggle, it was so hard to explain what was actually happening. I had been entertaining those policemen for my safety, for safety of my body parts. When I was about to speak more, she hung up. Those policemen smiled at me, then smiled at each other. I smiled too. They asked me to proceed with the story. I resumed, one policeman helped me to know where the story had reached. Minutes passed, then hours, my story kept on going. When I finished, the dusty clock on the wall indicated it was midnight. One policeman had laughed, two other had discussed the story, the man in the vest had kept his eyes on me and told me I had an interesting love story. He gave me his number and asked to call in case I ever faced any threat from police in pursuit of my love. Suddenly I felt very powerful, it was really strange, but I felt like a big underworld DON who owns the police in his pocket. Later they told me I was free and that was the real moment of relief. I shook hands with all the policemen, gave a nasty look to the man who had beaten his wife. The man in the vest asked me where my house was. They discussed among themselves that it was highly improbable to find a bus or an auto rickshaw at that time. I thought the same, but still I was not worried. I would be out of police station where I was brought for physical torture, what else I could ask for. I would barely mind spending the night in some park, even on the road. Suddenly I saw the man in the vest putting on his uniform and with no more discussion he asked me to follow. First he walked up to the boundary wall, and then he engaged both his hands in peeing. Seeing him do it in open, I felt the urge and the pressure. I walked up too, engaged both my hands, it was clearly a burning piss. A mishap is capable of warming up everything. So my police station experience ended up with tea, a bit of terror and a leak. So finally there was no cake cutting and definitely no birthday bumps. Now was the time for a bullet ride, actually the policeman's motor cycle. I thought of calling my brother, I needed help to keep the door open. I managed to break his sleep after fifteen minutes of continuous calling. Half an hour of ride at eighty km per hour, I reached. I got off from the pillion carefully, thanked the policeman who zoomed off within seconds; I stretched both my arms horizontally. I was finally home. When I headed towards the door in style I caught sight of my father who stood on his balcony. Another big trouble had come my way. He had witnessed it all, a policeman dropping me home. Again I had to think of something for this fresh mess. I had saved my life from a danger and now there was someone ready to swallow me. I conjectured a question-answer round with my father only in the morning as it was less likely that he was going to disturb himself at such an odd hour. I opened the door; it was totally dark as all the lights were off. There was no point in turning any light on. My room had been on ground floor and I could easily walk in darkness. I took a few silent steps, suddenly I heard the word "wait" and with that a light was turned on. I saw my father at some distance. I could sense dizziness in me, my mouth dried up, and I had not wanted to face him at that time, not at all.

"If I am not wrong you were at Nitish's birthday party? Right?" He asked in a thick tone.

"Right." I replied in a very thin tone.

"So who was that policeman?" He asked and made a face that showed his interest in hearing my answer. I thought to fabricate something but failed.

"I believe you have heard my question well." He said quite more seriously. I felt the need of opening my mouth before he came up with his judgment on the whole scene.

"He was Nitish's brother." I said.

"Nitish's brother is a policeman?" He enquired. His face looked confused.

"Yeah he is." I said.

"I guess you had told me earlier that he runs a BPO consultancy." He said raising his eyebrows. Hours of exhaustion had taken a toll on my thinking capacity, I blanked out completely. But I had to say something. Otherwise, my silence would have given him enough hints about the reality. With great endeavor, I made myself ready with something to say.

"Well basically he is a policeman but he runs a BPO consultancy too." I said with a little ignorance.

"How is that possible?" He asked and gave me a look full of irritation and disgust.

"I will explain, being an honest police officer means making only pennies. So he runs a BPO consultancy for obtaining some extra income. Most of the policemen are entering into this consultancy thing. The other big advantage is that they always have a backup." I stopped but the last line I spoke made no sense so it was no way convincing. My father gave me a "WHAT NONSENSE" kind of expression. I needed to make a better try.

"Backup? Well backup because in case an honest policemen is tainted of corruption charges and if he loses his job out of suspension, he will still have a backup carrier in BPOs. Besides a policemen's job is so full of intricacies, catching someone at the airport, beating those who have beaten their wives. It's just so awful. BPO is a much better option. You talk and only talk." I knew I was talking nonsense but couldn't afford to stop.

"You better catch some sleep now." He said in disgust and turned off the light. I was again in dark and again I felt a huge sense of relief for the second time that night. I went straightaway to the bathroom for a long shower. Now I thought about Shreya; I had been missing her badly. I had only wanted to hear her captivating voice. One hour passed; it had been a long wait before my phone rang . I reached for my phone quite like a lunatic. Without even checking the screen I picked and said "Shreya". "Rohan are you still with those policemen?" she asked quite frantically. "No, now I am home." I said casually. Then I told her everything that happened. She heard it but said she did not buy it all. I had to actually swear by all the gods in heaven to make her believe in me.Next moment, I received tip-offs about the pressure cooker tense situation on her side.

"It looks quite tense at this time. I have no clue how to handle this." She said. I thought for a minute while she spoke. I was trying to use my reckoning skills to come to a quick solution for resolving the matter. Soon I was sure about what was best in the situation.

"Make your mom and dad understand that there is nothing between you and me and in fact I was just a mistake which you have realized well now ." I sounded like I gave her an order.

"What?" She asked raising her voice up.

"Look at this time. It is the best thing to do because I want you to be here with me. When time comes we will handle all, convince all with right kind of strategy and plan. And trust me we will do it for our love." I explained.

"Do you feel it will work?" She asked. "There is no denying that it won't, but you should know I have a tie-up with policemen so I can think of doing other things too. So get youself chilled," I said to release all the tension that was building up.

"You are …" she said and laughed.

"I am the best, right." I said.

"Oh yes you are… who else can fool dangerous looking policemen so tactically?" She said like she was proud of me. I laughed. Now she was upset over what had happened at the airport. She turned grumpy again. Man, it's damn difficult to keep a girl happy for long. I joked with her and asked if she felt bad when her father caught my shirt because it was her exclusive right. I made more attempts to cheer her up. I pressed my cell phone harder on my ears to hear the sound of her laughter.

"You never allow me to be sad." She said.

"I am just doing my job well," I replied.

"Well then, keep up the good job!" She laughed some more.

600 KM FOR A KISS

One week passed, Shreya had succeeded in making her parents understand that their daughter had no interest in me. Although her father expressed so many doubts over it. How could she change altogether in such a short time, He must have really known that people in love don't give up so easily and they fight till the very end. He must have been dubious because of our very smart move but he had no other option than to believe in his daughter if she herself made it very clear that she did not love any guy. So finally they were cocksure that they really had no threat from a guy who was capable of running away with their daughter in case he decided to do so. So there was no point that she stayed in Varanasi for even a day more, besides she had been missing her classes as well. Finally she came back; it was a real big surprise that she gave me by keeping me on tenterhooks about the day she was reaching and I only got to know it when she was finally here. She had learned the style of springing surprises from me. We decided to meet the same day. My father had not been in Delhi so the car was all mine, I was tired of going out with Shreya in metro trains and auto rickshaws. When I left I realized, it was an unusual meeting and should have been different. We were meeting after facing a disaster. To work on the surprise factor I straightaway drove to a bakery and ordered a chocolate mud cake. It was not her birthday but it was surely a good day for our love. Congo Rohan & Shreya, the cake read.

I placed the square box with the cake on the back seat. This time I was going to pick her up from where she lived. After facing so much trouble, all our fear had taken a dive. I reached where she was waiting and my exhilaration was at its peak, I was almost dancing in my driving seat. At first I drove past her just to tease and in retaliation she turned her face away even after seeing me. When she got inside the car I drove looking at her. I would surely have rammed into some vehicle but she pushed my face with her right hand so that I looked straight. When again I turned my head towards her, she did the same thing laughingly. In one less crowded area, I braked and we stopped. It was the time for celebration and I reached for that square box on the back seat. She gave me a surprised look.

"What now"? She asked.

"Celebration time," I replied as I opened the box. I gave her a few seconds to read out what was written on the cake and her cheeks reddened like a tomato as she smiled. She was speechless. Now cutting the cake was not possible on the front seat so we moved to the back seat. The cake was placed between us. She smiled continuously. Together we cut the cake, then I ate from her hand and she ate from mine. Quite deliberately

I made the cake touch her nose; only a nitwit would avoid doing something of this sort on such occasions. She opened her mouth to make a haw sound. Then she counter attacked at me. She grabbed a bigger piece and flapped on my face without facing any kind of protest from my side. In reflex, I removed the cake that lay between us. I then moved close to her, we kissed. One small kiss followed by a big one, big and wet.

1 YEAR LATER

College life ended. Nitish and Satish followed me on the rickety path of CA after I persuaded them for months. I narrated my big plans of setting up a firm on qualifying and they were keen on being partners. Plus, girls were always an objective to meet, and they hoped to come into the purview of some smart bespectacled girls as they had had a harrowing time chasing glamourous dolls, the term was totally their own discovery. Shreya was showing some brilliance in fashion designing. Recently she got a chance to work under a very famous designer, on one project, and she got a lot of appreciation in her work. Once she showed her designs to me as well, I had been stunned, no wonder she had the skits of a designer and not of a doctor. Had her father remained adamant on seeing her a doctor, he would have played with a lot of lives. I am sure she would have used her scissors to create designs inside human body, so no chance of a patient surviving after the operation. Anyways, Shreya owned a car now and it was hers. The danger man had somehow felt that his daughter deserved a four wheeler and so he gifted her a brand new white Maruti Ritz. The car was for his daughter, the daughter was for me, so the car was for me. Congratulate me for getting a car so easily. But anyways a car is always something that comes as a gift from a father in law. For me it came long before. Okay, I am sorry I should stop being so mean now. BT now I used less of my father's four wheels. I must also tell you that I had begun to go to a musical institute where I learned singing, Shreya pestered me pretty hard and I could not keep off. She had strong faith in my singing potential. And that happened not so in favor of my father as I began irritating him with my early morning gargles and practices. During the morning when he would engage himself in deep yoga, I did my practice on a harmonium. This is the time when we exchanged "I can sing", "You just can't sing" looks. I would throw at him the first one and he would throw the second. But things were much better now. We no longer had a bride- father in law relationship. My doing well in chartered accountancy kept him happy, though I always wondered if a chartered accountant could compete with a doctor. Prashant continued to torture me in my thoughts. Shreya elucidated that a comparison was not required. My performance needed to be upto snuff and only that mattered.

TIME FOR MANICURE AND PEDICURE

"Rohan.. Guess what?" Shreya said during one of our regular chit chat sessions on phone at night. She was overflowing with excitement.

"You have bought a new brand of cologne." I guessed using all my past experiences. Every day she bought something and asked me to guess what she had bought on that day. That is the natural behavior of girls, actually girlfriends. .Quite regularly, they give you details of their new moisturizer or their new carrying bag as if we are required to make a journal entry on the transaction. For all non commerce background students I will elucidate. A journal entry is passed to make a record of a transaction. It is based on the same debit credit rules that I believe you already know. Don't forget how I messed up in Mrs. Kulkarni's lecture. Anyways my guess went down the plug. It was something else. Thank god.

"I think I should give up. You know I am so bad with making guesses." I said. And yes Of course, I could not have named every single product of a girl's use.

"I have told bhai about you." She said like it was a joke, a real good joke that you crack and expect others to enjoy it.

"What? What did you tell him?" I asked. Her words bamboozled me.

"I told him about you. That we kind of like each other". She said, again quite casually.

"You are serious?" I asked.

"Yeah. I had been waiting for a chance. So tomorrow you are meeting him at Hilton hotel. We have already booked a table for four." She announced and my heart bounced.

"Who is the fourth one?" I enquired. It would be very intimidating for me if the danger man was also going to join us. I was sure if that happened, I would walk out of the hotel all naked. Last time her father had failed to own my t-shirt. This time he would surely succeed, plus her brother was also there to fight for my trouser or jeans.

"The fourth one is bhabi." She said joyfully. "She too wants to meet you." She then began coaching to me on things that I needed to keep perfect. Getting hair trimmed and stubble in shape, proper cleansing of face, right kind of clothes, nothing like dandyish, keeping a pretty neat expression on face, many more included in her list. I asked her if I was required to get manicure and pedicure done too. She laughed at my exasperation.

AT HILTON WITH HITLER

I looked like a gentleman as if I was going to negotiate a nuclear deal. A pure white shirt over white vest and grey trousers, a pair of light brick red tape shoes that complimented my attire. Shreya had been my designer for the day; she had asked me strictly to go for a complete formal look. I hated formals but I had no choice. I bought a very costly Pierre Cardin pen for her brother and two triangles of Toblerone chocolate for the lady (her sister-in-law). I picked this idea of pen and chocolate to make a fantastic start in the pursuit of impressing her family. I was sure that Shreya was going to like it.

I reached comfortably on time. After receiving Shreya's green signal, I took the basement lift. When I reached, they all had their eyes on me. Eyes of the two females did not really bother me but her brother's gaze surely made me dizzy. They all welcomed me with a smile and I smiled too in response as I pulled an empty chair for myself. For the next few seconds we all looked at each other for no good reason, it was really very awkward for me. Her brother had put on a light colored shirt and had the gentleman's look whereas his wife looked very elegant in her Indian outfit. Shreya had worn a very long black dress and I had barely seen her in such kind of a princess outfit before. So she was the princess, I was the prince. I needed to feel confident, very confident.

"This is for you sir." I slowly kept before him the Pierre Cardin box that was gift wrapped colorfully. They were all caught by surprise and I noticed that. Then I gifted the lady with the chocolate that was packed too and now Shreya was dumbfounded.

"You have presents for us." Her brother said as he looked at his wife.

"Can we open this if you don't mind?" He asked for my permission but before I gave them my approval, they began opening their respective packets.

"Pierre Cardin! Good choice." He said as he opened the cap and tried the pen on waste gift paper. He then put the pen in the front pocket of his shirt. We all shifted our gaze to his wife who now had her chocolate in her hands.

"Thanks for this." She said. I accepted her thanks quite cheerfully.

"Does he know you are chocoholic?" Her brother said to his wife.

"But I am definitely unhappy with your choice in her case." He said as he looked at me. My heart beat quickened in that one precise moment.

"You see if you assume this job of giving chocolates to her, what am I supposed to give her? Charcoal?" He said and burst into a noisy laughter. The two women laughed too. I was not sure about whether to laugh or not but now I had understood that it was nothing serious. I laughed but it was not that natural. Shreya had flashed smiles at me quite consistently to make me feel comfortable and it surely helped.

"I think we should order something Chinese or Italian." He asked me. It left me puzzled. I neither fancied Chinese nor Italian. In fact I had barely tasted Italian food before other than pasta. I had completely no taste for Chinese.

"I would actually prefer South Indian. One masala dosa." I spoke with clear hesitation.

"Oh I am sorry; I so detest south Indian cuisine that I did not even give you a choice,my bad ."

It was a clean comment on my taste and that comment was bad. Shreya looked at me with pity in her eyes. They ordered for themselves a variety of Chinese and continental. I realized Hilton served a mammoth masala dosa and I was really going to have a tough time eating it. I regretted my South Indian food preference soon.

"So Rohan, how many times have you flunked in Chartered Accountancy? I mean you should have qualified by now." He attacked, quite openly and badly this time. I looked at my spoon full of sambhar which was very close to my mouth and dropped it back into the bowl. Shreya chewed her food in a very slow motion, I was being chewed by her brother. Her eyes were fixed at me and her ears waited for a sensible answer from me.

"Sir I was not sure about doing CA. I joined it late but now I am doing pretty well and I will soon qualify." I answered quite boldly. Thankfully he did not comment on my defense. I focused back on the pieces of pumpkin in my sambhar.

After a few minutes, I again looked at her brother to check if he was preparing to attack me again. This time I noticed something that almost stopped my heart, something unimaginable. The bottom of the pocket of his 'sea green' shirt had turned 'sea blue' and on noticing more I found it was wet too. That Pierre Cardin had secreted all the ink in his pocket, I almost fainted at that sight. I felt like emptying the whole big yellow layer of masala dosa and hiding my face with it. I began crying from inside and only I could hear its sound. Sweat beads emerged on my forehead even in air conditioned space. Suddenly Shreya gave me a glance with her head buried in her plate. By putting a very bad kind of expression on face I caught her whole attention, her eyebrows pulled each other. Using her face she asked me if everything was ok. Using my face I conveyed her that nothing was actually ok. I slowly used a finger to show her the ink on her brother's shirt. When she actually saw her brother's front pocket drenched in ink, she dumped her fork into the plate and it made noise. Then she turned into one of Gandhiji's three monkeys by covering her mouth with both hands. She remained in that posture for a few seconds and she only removed her hands to lean forward for a closer view, then she covered her mouth again. I held my chair tight, smacked my lips and felt like getting up and running away. But I had to face it in any case. Now before that ink dropped on his trouser or covered more areas on his shirt, we needed to tell him about it. I signaled Shreya to go ahead and give a shock to her brother so that he could further give me a bigger shock.

"Bhai…"

"Hmm what? You need something else?"

"No nothing…"

"Bhai…"

"Yeah what?"

"Your shirt?"

"What my shirt?"

"Your shirt…"

"My shirt…"

"Yeah…"

"Oh Shit!" He shouted.

He pulled the pen out of his pocket and threw it on the table.

"How did that happen?" His wife asked as she swallowed a Manchurian dumpling.

"I think you should go to the washroom." Shreya gave the best advice. At that moment I did not bother about anything else but I just had no courage to face him. Her brother got up in disgust and walked towards the washroom. I was not sure about what to do, whether to cry or laugh. Suddenly I realized the situation would get better if I helped him. So I left my seat too and followed him. I stopped for a few seconds before entering the washroom. Inside it was going to be a very bad scene, a horrifying one. I saw him standing in front of the full body mirror and touching the ink on his shirt with his fingertips. I froze completely and had a strong urge to pee for a bit of relaxation. But I had a job at hand. I plunged and moved ahead with my handkerchief in hand as I avoided looking into his eyes.

"Sir, let me try please." I said. Then I began rubbing on his shirt with my handkerchief, up and down, down and up. My heart jumped up in my chest, the ink on his shirt spread more, much more than before. The way he looked at me it was as if I had stabbed him so badly that now he would fall pointing his finger at me.

"Sir this is nothing I will do it, can u please take out your shirt off, it will allow me to rub better."

"What?" His expression worsened.

"I mean it will help me in cleaning it sir."

He took off his shirt and gave it to the laundry man who was unfortunately me. I held his shirt in my left hand and I used my right hand fingers to squeeze the ink out of his shirt. I did it so tightly that the ink between my fingers became tiny droplets and scattered into the air. I stopped and looked up, His face was full of ink, and I was dead this time. It was the pinnacle of disaster. Final aggravation. Nothing could be worse than this.

"Can I have my shirt back?" He asked in anger.

I said nothing and gave it to him out of fear. He put on the shirt, cleaned his face and left. I looked at myself into the mirror and looked down on the floor for the next few minutes. When I got my senses back I realized they all would be waiting for me. I came out staggeringly but found no one at the table. Even my masala dosa plate was removed.

KORBO, LODBO, JEETBO
Kolkata Knight Riders vs. Delhi Daredevils

This was my chance to improve my tattered impression in the eyes of her family. Shreya had again done something so that I could tag along with them to catch the live action of Kolkata Knight Riders vs. Delhi Daredevils in Feroz Shah Kotla Stadium. My first face to face with them turned out to be a mishap of a disastrous sort. It surely looked like an uphill task to face them with confidence. I told Shreya there was no use of hurrying, however, the fact of the matter was that I really didn't have the nerve to meet his brother. Though I was not completely wrong, her father was not going to force her to marry someone the next day. But a girl always has to do things the way she wants. Her father was after my blood already and now her brother took me as someone terribly mad. So there was no possibility of Shreya sitting like a spectator. If Hitler developed a liking for me our path was as smooth as the skin of an infant. She had given me hundreds of clarifications and she believed it was possible to get him on our side. I didn't believe her. Hitler was highly intractable from the way he behaved.

We were against eloping in case her family did not like me and perhaps that is why we had begun to grapple with all possible problems. They were only two, Hitler and the Danger man.

The game of cricket was now getting involved into all this. She had tried hard to convince her brother for being comfortable with my joining them to watch Kolkata Knight Riders vs. Delhi daredevils live clash.

Quite true, her brother was in fact more than a devil and I had to be someone craving to ride away with the girl I loved. So I was easily the rider. The job at hand was something like the rider desperately needed to impress the devil. But the devil was monstrous and the rider could feel like a chicken in the butcher's hand .

No goof ups, no howlers, there was no room for such things at all. I spent hours in preparing myself for a normal appearance before her brother and it was obvious to get late. Shreya had already called me a hundred times. She stopped only when I told her I had almost reached. The Feroz Shah Kotla stadium was jampacked with thousands of cricket crazy spectators.

The moment came and I found myself with them. I was welcomed by three different kinds of smile. Shreya's smile was mainly a delicious dish full of love and encouragement. Her sister-in-law's smile was plain in taste with a little concern and a lot of tease. Finally the smile of the Hitler, which was clearly a sneer of contempt and irritation.

I reciprocated with a smile which was full of embarrassment. Then I collapsed on my seat next to Shreya to feel at least minimal comfort. Our seating arrangement was like Hitler and I were on extreme ends, the two ladies acted as barriers between us which was for good in my view. Soon there was a discussion over the big clash between Kolkata Knight Riders and Delhi Daredevils.

Hitler and Shreya casted their support in favor of Delhi Daredevils as they were fans of Sehwag. This happened against my wish as despite having a weakness for KKR owner Shahrukh Khan's movies, I would have chosen to support the same team as Hitler with the hope of something positive happening for me.

"Korbo Lodbo Jeetbo." Hitler's wife said while she pointed a finger at me. So now Hitler and I were opponents (earlier I talked of something like devils vs. rider). Delhi won the toss. Hitler was clearly frenzied because Sehwag was on the field with his bat. KKR's most dangerous bowler Brett Lee got off to a great start with a maiden over. Right on this, Hitler's wife forced me with her eyes to join her into the chanting of *Korbo Lodbo Jeetbo* and I did it half heartedly, of course Hitler was not enjoying our teaming up.

The next two overs went really well for the Daredevils with Sehwag hitting mighty ones into the crowd. Hitler jumped up on his seat to dominate me mentally. He gave me a rough expression after producing terrifying noises to the best of his freaking ability. This continued for the entire batting of the Delhi Daredevils. I pretended to enjoy saying *Korbo Lodbo Jeetbo* as it was not politically correct to upset Hitler's wife. Hitler abhorred it clearly every time I opened my mouth.

Shreya and I kept on exchanging words; she desperately wanted me to get along well with her brother which did not seem possible.

Finally something happened during the fourth over which changed the whole equation between Hitler and me. KKR star Gautam Gambhir was on a roll after hitting two consecutive fours that raced through the extra over. It was the same over when Hitler busied himself on his phone. On the last delivery of the over, Gambhir went a few steps down the crease and connected so flawlessly that the ball vanished into the air for a few seconds. He played that stroke in our direction and only my eyes were fixed on the match as the two ladies had begun to discuss the recipe of an Italian pasta dish. It took me a second to realize that the ball was travelling towards the crowd of our side and another half second to actually believe that Hitler was going to get hit if he didn't move. I moved from my seat, kept my eyes on the ball, and I took an unbelievable catch exactly when my back faced Hitler. After the catch when I turned back to face him, Hitler held his phone a few inches away from his right ear and his face was a perfect example of a man in a state of complete shock. The two women watched me with their eyes full of disbelief and I knew that this was the moment of my victory. I threw the ball off and soon I showed up on the big screen for a few times. The crowd around us appraised me for the catch. Shreya was giving me looks that said the job was done. Hitler was still tight lipped but it was not the right time to ignore one thing, I had saved his nose from a hard cricket ball. The moment came when he called me to sit next to him. He asked me if I really loved his sister. I gave him a bold yes.

Another six was hit by the KKR side and they were easily ruling the roost. Devils were pushed on the back foot. Without wasting a second, Hitler chose to say what I wanted to hear from all my heart. He said he liked me and now he would stand on our side. Of course he made clear that my career mattered a lot. At last he thanked me for saving him from being injured, I smiled. So finally KKR had won. The two women were surely eavesdropping on us. When I threw a glare at Shreya, I found a different kind of happiness on her face. Even Hitler's wife gifted me a smile at my accomplishment. I was overjoyed. As we walked out of the stadium along with hundreds of people, Shreya took me by great surprise when she grabbed my arm and gave me an enveloping hug. Of course Hitler and his wife had moved ahead of us. Hundreds of people watched our embrace and so I hesitated, but then I felt her rush of affection. I threw my arms around her. We did it!

www.ingramcontent.com/pod-product-compliance
Lightning Source LLC
Chambersburg PA
CBHW051650260626
47170CB00004B/1432